THE PLACE WE GO TO IN BETWEEN

BRETT NOLAN

There are many people who helped me on this journey to finish this book and it would not be where it is today if not for them. Thank you to Michele Beuerlein, Alex Knode, Ben Dudley, Rachel Fenech, Jeff Ward, Eduardo Villa, Bradley Ross, my parents, Golnoush Pak, and Frances Pacheco. Your support helped me more than you would realize. And a special thank you to Mark Z. Danielewski whose book *House Of Leaves* was the main inspiration for this story. And to Neil Gaiman whose Masterclass kept me going.

ISBN: QZ-J6D-23-00064

Acknowledgements

Golnoush Pak - For designing the amazing cover art
https://www.instagram.com/goldfishsketches

Ben Dudley - For your extensive and critical editing and feedback

Michele Beuerlein - For your extensive editing and feedback

Alex Knode - For your extensive editing and feedback
https://www.instagram.com/alexknode

Rachel Fenech, for her editorial skills and insights on Shakespearean English.
https://www.linkedin.com/in/rachel-fenech-481a a3204

During Covid, I rediscovered my love for reading, and through reading I discovered my love for writing. Though I started a few stories before this, this is my first story that I finished. I am glad I had made time to finish it around my already complex and busy schedule. I have many more coming on the way so if you enjoy the story I had created, keep a lookout for these other ones coming. The ones currently in progress are:

The Pipe Systems Up North
Mary, Bishop, And Tom By The Sea
The Journey of Melanie
A Death at Disneyland
Unnamed story

I would love any feedback you would have on this story, whether good or bad. You can leave in the form of a review on Goodreads, Amazon, any other bookstore this book will be available at, or email me personally at BrettNolanWriting@gmail.com

Table Of Contents

THE PLACE
WE GO TO
IN BETWEEN

BRETT NOLAN

Chapter 1

I wake up and find myself surrounded by steep dunes that block my view of the horizon in all directions. There is sand beneath me and on my sides, but, to my surprise, there is none sprinkled on top of me. I stand up and dust off the back of my coat and pants.

Okay, what's the last thing I remember? I was heading to work on Madison Avenue. I remember two taxi drivers arguing with each other as I was crossing the street on the corner by the Sabrett stand. I stepped on the sidewalk and then— That's the last thing I remember. How could I have gotten here? Why am I here?

I don't hear waves crashing in the distance so I assume I'm not next to a coast. Must be a desert then.

Had I been drugged? Roofied? Was I kidnapped and dropped off here? If I was, why would they leave me here? Furthermore, what would be their reasoning for kidnapping me? I am of no value. Am I on some sort of sadistic show that sends people out into the desert to fend for themselves without their consent or knowledge? It would be hard to hide a camera here, though.

The dunes around me are all unscathed by human interaction. No tire marks in the sand. Not a single imprint around except for where I was laying and the few footsteps I have made so far. I obviously did not walk here. Maybe a helicopter dropped me off, but I hear no sound of one in the distance. In fact, I hear no sound at all. Not even the sound of a faint breeze coming by and brushing against my hair. The only thing audible is the sound of my tinnitus.

I pull my sleeve back to read my watch. The hands say that it's 7:55. I'm assuming that's a.m. by how bright it is. However, it doesn't appear to be 7:55 in the morning either. It's far too bright out. I don't see the sun overhead, so it must be hidden behind one of these dunes, though I don't see any shadows to indicate which. It is as if the sun is beaming down from directly overhead, as there's not a single trace of shade besides directly under my foot as I raise it off the ground ever so slightly. My watch is set to East Coast time, and I don't believe there's a single desert on the East Coast. The nearest desert to me is a long distance away. Texas? No, I don't believe their deserts look like this. The closest one like this would be in California.

Okay James, think. You've watched survival shows, you could get out of this. What supplies do I have? I reach into one pocket to find my cell phone with a newly shattered screen. I try to turn it on, but a flashing light signifies a dead battery. "Great," I say to myself out loud. I reach into my other coat pocket and feel nothing. My wallet is in my pants, but a credit card can't get me far here. At least they can ID my body if I were to drop dead.

Maybe there's someone nearby in the same situation as me.

"Help!" I cry out. I scream multiple times at the top of my lungs in multiple directions, yet no response calls back. I guess it's just me here.

I hesitate for a moment while standing there and looking at the massive dune in front of me. I then lift my leg and extend it forward. As I step down, I hear the sound of sand crackling beneath me. It gives me a confusing sense of relief. The only thing audible.

I begin climbing up a dune toward the very top. Every step I take, I listen for any sound that isn't caused by my interaction with this place. Something, anything. I beg for it to cry out to me. There is none. This silent landscape haunts me.

After climbing what must have been a hundred feet, I reach the top of the dune. In front of me, more dunes stretch out like a yellow sea, reaching well past the horizon. The waves on the left and right of me also went on without end. I turn around and notice behind me that the dunes start to disperse far off in the distance. At their furthest reach, I notice something. Something green. It's not too large, but it's definitely something. I'm not sure what, though. It has to be a day's travel at least.

I descend back down the dune and begin climbing the first dune between me and the isolated patch of green.

Chapter 2

I have been walking for what feels like hours. I've lost count of how many dunes I have passed. I stopped counting after I reached 20, and that was a long while ago. I check my watch again to see how much time has passed. 7:55. The hands haven't moved at all. Damn it. A broken watch.

At this point, my feet ache and are blistering. These loafers are not made for walking. They're not made for comfort either, apparently. If I had known I was going to be in a desert today, I would've definitely dressed quite differently.

I pause for a moment to catch my breath. I wipe the cascade of sweat from my forehead and wipe it on my sleeve. I must've sweated my body weight by now. With my loafers causing more and more discomfort, I stop to take them off, hoping I can walk the rest of the trek barefoot. I lift one foot out of its shoe and lower it to the ground, screaming out in pain as the sand scorches my skin. I reluctantly put my shoe back on and start trudging again.

One step, two steps. One hundred steps. I begin counting the steps to occupy my time. At one point, I start singing songs from my mental playlist. I sing any songs that come to mind: "Blackbird" by The Beatles, Tupac's "Hit 'Em Up," and even "Mambo No. 5" by what's his name.

The voice in the back of my head keeps telling me to just stop. To give up. Something that is always festering in the back of my head. The only thing keeping me going is seeing the green getting closer and closer with each dune I pass. Unfortunately, I still can't make out what it is. I assume it's trees. Palm trees, possibly. If that's the case, there could be water. At the very least, there could be shade. A place for me to escape this dreadful sun. That'll be great. For all I know, however, it could be a billboard advertising Sprite. There's some great traffic out here.

I have no clue how far away the green truly is. I speculate that it's 10 miles away, but it doesn't look like it's getting any closer.

I hope my wife is alright. I doubt she's in this same predicament as me. The last time I saw her was when I was leaving for work. As I was grabbing my coat, I said goodbye to her.

She either didn't notice my comment or ignored it. Thinking back, I didn't see her face the entire morning. Only the back of her head as I walked out. She was in the kitchen, on her phone. Doing what, I'm not sure. Typical morning, though.

They say you should travel the desert at night and rest during the day, but I don't believe I have the luxury of resting now in my situation. Besides, I haven't seen any sign of it becoming dusk anytime soon. The glare off the sand is just as bright as before.

I decide that I am too exhausted to go any further. Maybe resting my eyes for a bit won't hurt. I take my coat off and lay down, draping my coat over my chest and around my head to protect my skin from the sun and the scorching sand. I close my eyes. I pray that this is all a terrible dream and that, when I wake up again, I'll be back in my apartment in New York. I'll wake up to the sound of a taxi blaring its horn down below where the worst thing I have to worry about is oversleeping and being late to work. I'll walk into my kitchen where I'll see my wife. She looks at me, stands up, and says "Hello."

I jump awake. I heard someone say hello. I could've sworn it. I look around but see no one. The only footprints in sight are the ones I made. Did I just dream of that voice? I look at my watch instinctively. I should probably get moving. Though I have nothing to base it on, I feel like I rested for about 15 minutes. I'm still exhausted, but at least my legs received a little bit of a break.

As I stand up, brushing sand off my coat and pants, I hear it again. "Hello." This time, I know I've heard it. It wasn't coming from far away. Maybe right over that dune just ahead of me. It's a voice I don't recognize, but at least the person might speak English. They sound young.

I shouldn't make myself known before I see who it is. I'll head up the dune and get a good vantage point. They could be out to harm me. It could also be someone here to rescue me. They might have water or a vehicle. They could also have a gun.

As I'm climbing up the dune, I hear the voice again. "Dannie, this ain't funny. Where you at?"

It is the voice of a young man. He definitely seems to speak English. That will certainly help communication and narrow down where I am.

Each step I take closer to the top, the more the muscles in my legs burn and ache. Out of breath and pouring sweat, I reach the top, and, as I slowly peer over the other side, my imagination goes wild. Who could this person be?

The person that stands below me is none of the characters I had pictured in my head. Standing there right below the dune is a young white man wearing light blue above-the-knee shorts with a red Ohio State sweatshirt. He's looking off to the left. No equipment on him. Only the clothes on his back. I assume he has no water or food either. No weapon on him from what I can see, and he doesn't appear hostile or dangerous in any way – unless you're a drunk chick at a frat party.

I divert my attention away from him to examine his surroundings. There is a circle of his own footprints immediately around him, but none showing how he got here. Same situation as me.

In a soft tone, I say to him, "Hey." With no wind or other sounds nearby, my voice travels far.

Focused on scratching his beard, he is startled by the sudden noise. He turns his head toward the sound of my voice, eventually spotting me residing on top of the dune. His face quickly changes from concern to relief.

"Yo, how's it going? Have you seen my pals?"

I look around and say, "I don't think there's anyone but us around here."

He looks around too, then turns back to me. "Oh, trust me. They're near. They pull stuff like this all the time. One time, I woke up on my mattress in a lake."

"How did you get here?" I ask.

He just shrugs his shoulders. "I don't know, man. My buddies? What about you?"

"Not sure either."

I head down the dune to meet this person face to face. At the bottom, I get a better look at him. He's about 5'11. Beard is thin and slightly unkempt. Wearing a baseball cap with an Alpha Sigma Phi logo on it with the same color as his sweatshirt.

"I don't think your buddies dropped you off here."

"Okay, and what makes you say that?" he asks, mockingly.

"Look at the ground. Notice how the only footprints around are yours and mine. Unless your buddies can float, I don't think they brought you here. Also, your footprints don't come from anywhere either."

"Are you trying to tell me I fell out of the sky?"

"No, I'm trying to tell you I don't think this is a practical joke by your friends. I was in the same situation as you a few hours ago. I woke up with no trail of footprints showing me how I got here. I've been walking over dunes ever since."

"Damn, that sucks, man. Ayy, real quick, what's your name?"

I hesitate momentarily before saying, "James. And you?"

"Fasho, my name's Barry."

"Okay Barry, what's the last thing you remember?"

"Aww man. Last night I was at this rager on the Ohio State campus. Was way too turnt. I just came to like five minutes before you got here."

"Last thing I remember was heading to work in New York. Know any deserts that could be near us?"

"Huh, that's a good point. There are none anywhere near us. We're hella far, man," Barry says as he looks around. "How long was I out for?" he asks himself as he stretches his back.

"Do you have a phone?"

"Yeah man, but I forgot to pay my service last month so I need wifi to call. Don't suppose there's any around here."

"So your phone is useless?"

"Nah," Barry says as he jingles the phone in his hand. "It makes for a pretty expensive Casio if you ask me."

"Well, what time does it say on it?"

"11:58. What's it say on that nice watch of yours?"

"It's broken but it says 7:55. I think it's best to go off of your phone's time," I say to him. We can use it to keep track of how long we've been traveling."

"Travel?" Barry says confused. "Travel where?"

"I saw a patch of green over that way. Could be trees, which could also mean water, which could also mean people."

Barry touches his already chapped lips. "Water is good. Do I want to ask how far?"

"You should be able to see it once we climb to the top of that dune."

"Is it on the other side of the dune?" Barry asks, his voice hopeful.

"It is not," I respond back. "Many more dunes ahead before we reach it."

Barry lets out a sigh and begins stretching his legs.

"What are you doing?" I ask him.

"What? I don't want to get a cramp..."

We've been walking to the patch of green for about an hour. What it is, I still can't tell. Still a possibility it's a Sprite billboard. At first, Barry was fast-paced and determined. Taking the lead like it was a race. At one point, he was even about 50 paces ahead of me. I warned him that he should conserve his energy and walk at a slower pace, prompting him to call me a "sore loser" and a "pussy."

But now, Barry is struggling. He's fallen so far behind me that I have to stop for a moment to wait for him to catch up. I wait on top of a dune that mimics the many we have already passed and look ahead to our path forward. About ten dunes ahead, they begin to clear up and space out more. It should be an easier trek once we get there. We still have quite a distance to go, though.

I look back and find Barry finally reaching the top of the dune. He's panting, with his hands on his knees.

"Five minute break," he says between breaths.

"Fine. What's the time on the phone?"

He pulls out his phone and says, "11:58." He rubs the sweat off his forehead. "Have we been walking for 12 hours?" he asks confused.

"I think your phone is just broken."

"Oh well," Barry says as he tosses his phone off the dune. It makes a soft thunk as it hits the sand near the bottom.

"Why'd you do that?" I ask pissed off. "We could use it once we finally get somewhere."

"Relax Chief. We're walking that way anyways. I'll pick it up once we get to it."

Looking at his drenched sweatshirt, I ask him, "I'm guessing you go to Ohio State."

"Aww, no, man. I just go there for the parties. I dropped out of community college like a year ago."

"Why'd you drop out?"

"I'm just not made for college. I don't know."

"How come you're wearing that sweatshirt then?" I ask, while pointing at it.

"It's a great way to blend in. Ain't trying to get kicked out of the party."

"So what *are* you made for, Barry?"

"Bro, I'm made to party," he says with excitement in his voice and his arms raised in the air.

I turn around without responding and face our destination once again. Hard to believe I was in New York not too long ago. New York and here. No in-between. Even though this is the same Earth, this is a different world. At least to me.

I look over to see Barry, who still has his hands on his knees and his face pointed toward the ground. "We should keep moving," I tell him. "The green patch sure isn't going to head in our direction."

"We stop for a little break, and you really made me talk the whole time instead of letting me catch my breath," Barry says in an annoyed but comedic tone. "By the way, that was not five minutes."

We press on. Barry reaches for his phone in the sand and picks it up, immediately crying out in pain from its heat. Wincing, he places it in his pocket. "See, I told you I'd grab it. Nothing to worry about. And look, it still says 11:58."

I keep walking and stop paying attention to what he was saying.

It's probably been five hours since I've arrived here. This whole time, I still haven't seen the sun at all, even though it looks like high noon. This place is strange. This place could be my death. I won't die here, though. At least, I will try not to.

My whole body aches – from the blisters on the bottom of my feet to the jolts of pain in my back. Any skin not guarded from the sun is burnt and tender. The skin that is covered is chafed. My lips are chapped to hell, and my tongue doesn't have a single drop of saliva left to moisten them. All the water in my system has probably been sweated out.

I can tell Barry is feeling it as well. He is slumped over as he walks, dragging his feet slowly through the sand instead of lifting them. His previous white skin is now a harsh red. His skin burns to the touch as he wails out swear words every time he wipes the sweat from his forehead. Even with his hat on, he somehow managed to get burnt on his forehead. One time, I'm pretty sure I saw him trying to suck the sweat out of his sweater when he thought I wasn't looking. If my top wasn't pelted with sand, I'd consider the same.

Barry pauses in his tracks. "Man, I dealt with Ohio heat no problem, but damn, this is a whole new level." He sits down in the sand, ignoring the scorching heat on his exposed legs. He continues, panting between words, "Man... I really wished I stumbled... into a glacier... than here."

I give him my coat to lie on so he doesn't get burns on his skin. It's an expensive coat, but it's already ruined. "Thanks, man," he says. "I'm going to maybe take a little day nap for a quick sec if you're cool with that."

"Sure. Just make it quick. We have to keep moving." I would pressure him even more to press on, but I was in the same position hours before, right before I heard his voice in this quiet place. Drained. Exhausted. Feeling of helplessness. Though we weren't showing the latter, we both felt it. We both know the other felt it, but we chose to keep it to ourselves. There's not much optimism when you show up in a desert without any resources or recollection of how you got there. At this point, my only hope is that single splash of green in this expanse of yellow and blue.

We still don't know what's there, though. Blue and yellow make green on the color chart. That's what I learned in kindergarten. Maybe it is just the place where the blue sky and yellow desert meet. A mirage maybe. I could just be marching us to our deaths. Maybe Barry should lead us. Where else is there to go though? Every other direction just stretches on endlessly. They will certainly be the paths to our death as we go nowhere fast. At least this direction offers us a slight chance of hope. Who really knows the chance of us surviving this. Slim to none? Ten percent? Thirty percent? It doesn't matter. Knowing the percentage won't help. It would probably just discourage us even further.

I look down at Barry. Completely passed out. "Alright, you rested for about ten minutes. You should probably get up now. We need to keep moving."

"Fasho. Just give me a sec to get up."

Barry slowly gets up. He takes his time to prolong walking again as long as possible. I hear an array of cracks from his back and legs as he stands. Instead of taking a step, he continues the charade by stretching, over-exaggerating each motion to make it last longer. First by having his arms reach down to his shoes, followed by pressing his hands against his back, and cracking it.

"Are you done yet?" I ask unamused.

"I told you. Just give me a sec. I don't want to get a cramp." Barry takes off his hat to wipe the sweat off his face. He lets out a few swear words when he touches his skin again. From there, I notice his hair for the first time. It is brown, medium length but buzzed on all sides. He lets out a big sigh and looks around in his surroundings, hoping for some form of escape from here. He fully turns away from me and I notice a slash on the back of his head. Not a small cut, but a giant gash. The only thing I could let out of my mouth is "Oh my god!"

Barry turns around and lets out a concerned and confused, "What?"

I point my finger toward him and stutter out, "Your— Your head. Th— There's an enormous gash in the back of it."

Barry scoffs at me as he reaches for the back of his head. "What? No, there's not. The desert's got you— Oh damn. There's a giant gash back here, man."

"Does it hurt?"

"No. Not at all," he says with concern. "Is that bad it doesn't hurt?"

"I don't know. Let me take a look at it."

"Alright, Doctor," Barry says, tongue in cheek.

I get closer and examine the gash tearing through the buzzed hair on the back of his head. It is long and deep. Stretches diagonally all the way across the back of his head. It's perfectly clean. Not a speck of sand entered it with his tight cap covering it. No blood on the injury either, dry or wet. Looks fresh, though. Like it only happened moments ago. No evidence of scarring.

"There's, uh, no blood or sand in it," I say.

"Well, that's good, right?"

"Yeah, I think. We should put a covering over the wound to keep it clean."

"Ight. I'll use my socks," he says as he bends down to untie his shoe.

I quickly intervene. "How about something more sanitary?" I grab the inside of my coat pocket, rip it out, and hand it to him.

"Thank you," he says as he puts it over his wound.

"Are you finally ready to move?" I ask in an agitated tone.

He lets out a sigh. "Yeah, I guess so."

Chapter 3

I haven't been able to see the patch of green for quite some time. It has been obscured from our vision by the dunes in front of us. They have started spreading out more, giving us more space to walk around the individual dunes rather than having to climb each one like before. It requires more distance to cover but at least it saves us energy and time. If we were still climbing them, we would be at least 20 dunes back and way more exhausted. My thighs are thankful to have a break from the constant up and down, but they still bark in agony with each step. I have become so accustomed to walking on sand that I don't even notice it anymore. Much like sailors develop their sea legs, I now have my sand legs.

Our pace has slowed. We should stop soon, even if just for a few minutes. The light is still blazing in our faces. I beg for a little bit of a breeze to blow into my face and relieve my scorched skin, but this terrain still deny the existence of wind.

I wipe my forehead of the little bit of sweat still coming out of my body. The dune in front of us protrudes high above the dunes around it; it would be a steep climb to the top. I turn back to scorched Barry and say to him, "I think we should walk up this dune and scout how far we are from our destination. I don't believe we're too far now."

Barry says nothing. He responds by letting out a sigh and giving me a single nod of approval totally devoid of enthusiasm. He lays his hands on his legs as he catches his breath.

Being in this situation makes me feel better about my lackluster life back in New York. When I said I wanted to travel, this is not what I had in mind. I definitely can't see myself visiting any sort of desert environment in the future. Probably no more beaches either. I'll plan for the coldest climates I can find: Greenland, Sweden, Siberia.

I remember at one point Jasmine talked about wanting to go to Sweden. I wonder if she ever went. She always wanted to travel. Even got me to travel with her a bit with what little money we had. I always wonder what Jasmine's up to. That was such a long time ago. Back before I met my wife.

Being out here actually makes me miss my wife for once. I find myself imagining our reunion. I can see it already. I get off the plane. She's there, waiting for me just past security. She runs up and hugs me with glee and excitement in her eyes before she remembers that she really doesn't care for me at all. She'll say something like, "It's good to see you again." Then, once we return to the apartment that night, things turn back to normal. The next day, she barely looks at me. We barely engage in conversation, and we spend our time in separate rooms – her hiding in the kitchen while I camp in the bedroom.

I break out of my thoughts when I hear Barry's footsteps sneaking up behind me. I'm halfway up the dune without really realizing it. My thighs bring sharp pain and gets worse with each step. When I was walking on the flat sand, this pain was hibernating, but emerged from its slumber with a vengeance during my uphill trek. One step. Two steps. It's all excruciating. My entire body is begging me to stop.

I'm two-thirds up now, though. If I've climbed this far, I can make it to the top. I stop counting the steps as each one brings me further agony and paying attention to them just makes time seem slower than it already is.

Barry is still dragging behind me but isn't too far back. He looks down rather than forward. I can sense the defeat in him. How he is starting to give up hope to where even Tony Robbins can't motivate him.

At the top, the patch of green I've been following for hours and hours is once again in sight, not too far off. I can finally see what I've been chasing for so long. It's trees. Magnificent trees. Sweet shade from the sun. There are many of them. At least 50 bunched up against each other. One on top of the other, their overlapping branches creating a blanket of shade below. Barry trudges up behind me.

"My god, yes!" he cries out, breaking his silence.

The trees are around maybe half-a-mile away at this point. A straight shot of only flat sand and no dunes. The green patch sits in a crease between two hills that seem to hold a color just slightly differently than everything else around them. It's the first time I've seen anything other than sand here.

Knowing that soon we will have a bit of relief, we quicken our pace. I don't recognize these trees. Their unusual shape is like nothing I've seen before. A tall, thin canopy of branches lays flat on the top, blocking the sun from entering. Below the canopy, the trunks are bare and devoid of branches.

Each step I take closer to the trees feels easier and easier. I think, at first, it was more of my enthusiasm, but I look down to see the sand is being replaced by dry ground. My legs are slowly adjusting to the hardening surface, as I almost trip on myself a few times.

I'm nearly in front of the trees. Here, the ground is firm and hard. The dirt beneath my feet is dry and cracked, a sign that water hasn't touched this surface for ages. I couldn't care less, though. I'm given temporary shade as well as a harder ground to walk on. We can focus on water later. Just rest for now, a break from the sun.

I collapse to my knees once I reach the shade. My eyes shut as soon as my head touches the cool ground. Barry comes shortly after, flinging his body to the ground with a loud thud. I slowly open my eyes and look over to where he fell and see a cloud of dust surrounding him. He mumbles something before falling silent. I close my eyes shortly afterward.

Chapter 4

I wake up feeling like I've been in a deep sleep for hours. I don't exactly feel well rested, but I don't feel exhausted like before. When I stand up, my kneecaps crack and my spine shoots a spike of pain across my back. Stretching doesn't really seem to ease it. I yearn for coffee right now. Or at least caffeine in some form or another. I let out a yawn while rubbing my eyes as I look over towards where Barry had plummeted to the earth. Still unconscious, he hasn't moved an inch. I doubt he'll be awake for quite a while. I'll let him be for a bit. Let him wake up in his own time.

I walk around the perimeter of the trees to do some recon. We've made it to our objective. What's our next course of action? We can't survive solely on hard ground and temporary shade. There's no water visible, yet these trees are able to survive somehow. We need food, shelter, and civilization. I was raised to navigate a concrete jungle, not a sandy sea.

I look in the center of the grove to notice a tree with markings on it. I walk closer and see that someone has carved *ville* into it, followed by an arrow that points to the back of the grove. "A village," I think cheerfully to myself. Oh, thank god. If I had the energy, I'd dance around in glee. We're near hope, salvation, water, and food. French though. We must be somewhere in West Africa. Certainly a lot farther from home than I had hoped to be.

I follow the direction of the arrow. To the back left of the grove, I find a spot near the back where the two hills seem to meet. On further inspection, however, I see that the hills don't actually meet. In fact, both submerge into the ground before coming in contact with each other, creating a small dirt pass between them about ten feet wide.

As much as I do not want to leave the shade, I feel that I should scout and see what's ahead. I'll only walk forward about ten minutes. Walk ten minutes back. Twenty minutes, tops. I turn around to see Barry still unmoved. He lies perfectly still, his stomach subtly rising and falling with his breath. I'll be back before he wakes up. Definitely.

I take a step out of the protection of the shade and into the glaring heat. I start sweating on contact, realizing it's extraordinarily hotter than I remember it from before our rest. Hopefully, I can get reacclimated to this warmth.

These sandy hills in front of me hold no movement. Stripped and devoid of life. Just various shades of yellow and orange.

In the short time I've walked on this pass, I haven't been able to see too far ahead thanks to its sharp twists and blind turns. I haven't a clue how long the path will be. Could stretch for miles, or could end at the next turn.

Maybe I should turn back soon. I don't want Barry to think I abandoned him. He could end up taking off in a completely different direction. Plus, the dirt's not leaving footprints like the sand was. I'll return after this next corner up ahead. I'm coming back this way anyways.

I turn the corner to find that the winding pass between the hills has turned into a straight path. The hills end about 300 yards ahead. After that, it looks like flat, open terrain again. Hopefully not sand. The color is different. Rather than a light yellow, it has more of a brown hue. I can't see how far the landscape extends, though. Most importantly, I don't see any sign of a village or human life. Now that I think about it, I haven't heard any planes soaring through the sky during my entire time here. Must be nowhere near a flight path.

In the plain ahead, not far past the two hills, I notice something – a rectangular shape extending upward into the air. Whatever the light gray shape is, it clearly wasn't naturally made and sticks out like a sore thumb. It was made by someone and someone placed it there. Could be a sign pointing to the town. Signs aren't usually that big, though. I can't tell how big it is from this distance, but it has to at least be the size of a human.

I should go check it out. I take a step forward before I turn my head back. I should grab Barry first. He could just be waking up and noticing I'm gone. "I'm coming back this way, anyway," I tell myself outloud.

I arrive back at the grove to find Barry gone. "Crap," I tell myself out loud. I've only been gone twenty minutes – at least I think it was just twenty minutes. He couldn't have gone too far from here. I head out to the edge of the grove until I reach the sand. I see our footsteps from before but don't see any new ones have emerged. He couldn't have passed me on the trail I was on. I would've seen him. Might have gone left or right. Which direction should I—?

"Hey, how'd you sleep?"

I see Barry standing there. Half-awake and yawning, still sun-scorched as ever. All nonchalant.

"Where did you go?!" I ask him in a stressed tone.

"And a 'good morning' to you too," Barry responds. "I was off taking a piss behind those trees over there. I figured you trailed off to take a dump somewhere."

"I scouted ahead. There's a word carved on that tree which says *ville*. I followed the path it pointed at to see what was up ahead. I guess I was a little too eager."

"And?" Barry is suddenly interested.

"And what?" I respond.

"What did you see up ahead? Was there a town?"

"Oh. No, I didn't see a town. I saw a rectangle, though."

"A rectangle," he repeats, confused.

"It was something in the shape of a rectangle. Couldn't have been naturally made. Couldn't make out what it was. Wasn't too far off."

"You're out here making us chase colors and shapes, man," Barry says as he starts stretching his legs.

"Well, it got us this far. Besides, that thing is the first sign of humans here besides me, you, and that tree."

"True, a tree is promising us a town, and a tree hasn't lied to me before. I'm in."

"When were you ever out?" I ask, smirking.

As we walk through the hills, I take notice of the hills on each side of us. really trying to take in every single detail. Earlier, I was more focused on looking forward on the trail. Now that I'm looking more closely, however, the hills seem to lack any detail whatsoever. As much as I try to find something, I'm left staring at a blank palette. They almost look two dimensional. No sense of life on them. No little geckos. No tumbleweeds or small patches of plants. No little rocks or even pebbles scattered down their sides.

Barry's pace is more conservative than before. What he thought would be a quick endeavor has become a long excursion for him. Hopefully, we'll run into that town soon, and hopefully, they're friendly. Eventually, both of us will collapse and fall from exhaustion if we don't find food or water.

Barry breaks the silence. "How is the New York life? I've never been."

"I mean, it's alright. Busy, stressful. Loud."

"Wow, such a good storyteller."

"Well, I'm not really in a mood to tell you my backstory and frankly not in any mood to talk. Why don't you give yours then if you're in the mood to converse. What can you tell me about Ohio?"

"Yeah, actually I grew up in Cali, but moved to Columbus about four years ago."

"How come?"

Barry pauses for a second before responding. "My dad's work moved, so I went with him there. Now I'm crashing at a homie's house, working part time at a pizza place." Barry stops walking for a second. "Ah, shit. I missed my shift. I'm going to get fired forsure."

"Barry, that should be the least of your worries right now."

"Maybe you don't live paycheck to paycheck, Mr. New Yorker, but some of us do, Chief. And besides, you try having Mr. Risotto as a boss."

"You have a boss named Mr. Risotto?" I ask.

"His name is Mr. Rossi, but I call him Mr. Risotto." He laughs. "That must be why he hates me."

Ahead, I see the turn that revealed the straight path before. We turn the corner, and I tell Barry, "Look. That's the object I saw from before. What do you think it is?"

"If we're lucky, it could be a fridge."

"Who would leave a refrigerator out here?" I ask.

"Desert people," he responds quickly. "They're crazy, man. Name a movie with a desert person that isn't crazy as hell."

Before I could even respond with an answer, he says, "Exactly! None."

I ignore him and continue walking forward. The path is getting wider and wider as the hills disperse on either side of us.

My lips are dried and cracked. Skin is scorched and irritated. Feet blistered all over. I have been in discomfort for so long that my body has chosen to ignore it. I only notice it when I think about it, much like breathing. The only pain I can't ignore is the psychological pain. With each passing minute in this place, I grow more concerned about the fact that our fate may be sealed here. Each step we take that doesn't reach our objective makes that vision more of a reality and our hope stepping further away. This could be it. This could be the end. I have to keep pushing through, though. I do. Or do I really? Do I really need to keep going? What do I obtain if I keep going? More suffering? More pain? More heat? I could easily just stop and count my losses. Collapse from exhaustion right here, right now, and just have it be over with. What would I lose? A shitty job, a shitty apartment, a shitty life? The shitty life I settled with.

I could've done something to change it, but instead I settled for what I had. Made excuses to avoid putting effort into changing my life. Could've changed jobs, moved out of New York, got a divorce, but I didn't. All it would have taken was a little push. A little push I couldn't seem to muster.

Should I just stop? No, I can't stop. Especially when there's hope up ahead, no matter how little of it there is.

I look over at Barry. His situation isn't much better. Sweat is still pouring from his face. He pants heavily as he tries to catch the sweat drops to retain water. I assume that his feet are covered in blisters, just as mine are. Thoughts are surely similar as well.

At least I'm not alone here. As much as it's messed up to say, I'm glad I won't die here alone if it comes to it. I do not wish Barry to be in this dreaded situation, but him (or just about anyone else) being here puts me at ease, and I'm not sure why. How does that bring me comfort, though? I remember that scene from *Dirty Harry* where Clint Eastwood tells the jumper, "You want to take somebody with you when you go."

But why? Does the *we are all in this together* feeling ease the harsh realities of life? The knowledge that the experience you hold in that minute isn't exclusive to the ground beneath you or the death bed in which you lay. As your cries for mercy fall onto death's deaf ears, your screams of fear and agony cannot bounce off a living soul's eardrum. Who stands next to you as you go makes no difference. Barry, a homeless person, my wife who has no sense of re—

"Yo, Chief, that's a door."

Barry's outburst pulls me out of my trance. I realize I have been staring toward the ground for some time during my inner monologue. I look at him extending his arm, pointing to what lays in front of us. I turn my head to find that we are at the end of the pass and about to be met with a dirt plain. Dry and cracked, just like before. Barren of anything except for what stood in front of us a distance away. Straight vertical lines on each side, with a half dome on top.

It most certainly is a door. I see the handle, the frame, the detailing, everything. It's almost taunting us the way it stands there emotionless and without purpose. The only response I can give Barry is "Yeah" in an unsure, confused tone .

As he laughs, Barry says, "Desert people, man. They set up a door but forgot to install the building."

Each step we take brings us closer to the door but not closer to the mystery of why it's there. A door? *A door?* Why a door? Why on Earth is there a door here? Is this a convoluted prank? It has to be. Leaving us stranded in the desert just to find a door and a tree carving. A door to what? It's a door to nowhere. There's nothing even remotely resembling a building nearby. There's no other aspects here that are human-made. A door that has absolutely no purpose.

Barry laughs. "You know, if we survive this trip, man, no one is going to believe we saw a door out in the middle of the desert. No matter how drunk they are."

I don't respond, as I'm lost in my thoughts, trying to come to some sort of conclusion as to how this got here. Maybe it fell out of a cargo plane and landed perfectly upright and miraculously undamaged. Maybe a nouveau artist set it up as an art exhibit.

"How do you think it got here?" I ask Barry as we move closer to the door.

"It doesn't matter how it got here. What matters is that it is here," he responds back.

The door now stands about five feet in front of us. We stop to look closer. The door itself is composed of light gray wood planks. The frame that shells it is a darker gray – to the point that it's almost black. There are thin cracks between the wood planks that make up the door. Not enough to peer through but just enough to give notice that it is there. There's a long, thin latch hung on the right side of the door rather than a doorknob. It does not look like a modern door in any regard, but more like something you would see inside a castle or some other pre-Industrial Revolution building.

I inspect around the door as Barry does the same. I try opening the door with the latch but it won't move at all as I nudge it. It's either locked or jammed. I figure that sand or dirt must have gotten inside the lock system and damaged it. However, there's not one speck of sand on any part of the door. Besides some visible sun damage, this door seems unscathed by the elements and rather clean (apart from the fingerprints we have left on it). I forfeit trying to wrestle with this latch and hear Barry call out, "There's letters on top of the door frame." I look up and see what Barry is referring to. An engraving of the letters *A.C.* adorns the frame over the door, carved about a half-inch deep into the wood.

"What do you think A.C. stands for?" Barry asks.

"It could be the initials of the manufacturer of the door or the frame," I respond.

"It could also stand for *air conditioning.* Maybe there's one inside."

I go around back to inspect the other side of the door. Rather than seeing the other side of the door, though, I find that the frame engulfs the backside and covers the door in all but the front-facing direction. The frame is about six inches deep so there's no room for anything inside besides the door itself.

At the ground below the door, a shadow doesn't cast in any direction. I bend down and press my face against the hot dirt, peering under the frame. There's nothing to keep this door up but itself. A quick gust of wind could easily knock it to the ground. When I was messing with the latch, the whole thing should've easily fallen over. I wipe the dust off my cheek as I stand up. I give the door a little push and don't feel any give.

Barry catches on to what I'm trying to do, and, with a smirk, he says, "Here, let me give it a try. I played JV in high school." I move out of the way as Barry backs up about ten feet. He lets out an incomprehensible yell and charges for the door pretending to have a football gripped in his hand. With a loud bang, he is stopped dead in his tracks by the door. All the dust and sand on Barry puffs out into a cloud as he collapses to the earth at mach speed.

I rush over to Barry on the ground. "Are you injured?"

Barry grabs the shoulder he charged the door with. "Man, this door should play defensive line."

His comedic tone tells me he's not seriously injured. I look back up at the door and find that it is unscathed from Barry's charge. Not a single mark or imprint. No splintered wood at all, despite the planks on the door looking as if they have the strength of toothpicks.

"Barry, you didn't make a single dent in that door."

Barry rubs his shoulder as he says, "Man. Coach would chew me out if he saw me right now."

"Well, I guess we should keep moving," I say.

Barry, dusting sand off his shorts, responds, "What direction?"

I look around. The left and right of us stretch on indefinitely. With only the hills behind and a new set of them up ahead, I suggest "Straight?" with no confidence.

"That's reassuring," Barry responds.

We start moving along.

Chapter 5

The further we go, the more sand I notice below our feet. Every time I extend my leg, there's more sand to greet my foot than the step before. "Sand is starting to pick up again," I hear Barry call out.

I look up and see a dark object projecting above the landscape, rippling behind the heat waves. It's another door. It has to be. Can't make the details from here, but it has to be. It's at my 2 o'clock. Maybe half a mile away. Color is dark, rounded at the top. It's there. It definitely is.

Barry notices it shortly after I do. He stops dead in his tracks in front of me and points his finger out toward the black figure in the distance and says, "No. No. No. No. No. Bro, please tell me you don't see that."

"Do you think these are markers into the town?" I question myself more than Barry.

"I think they're markers to a creepy shack," he scoffs.

"Do you have any other suggestions on what should be our travel guide?" I ask, annoyed.

"I'm just not tryna follow some doors to my death, Chief."

"Every other direction here leads toward our death."

"Who would leave doors out in the desert? Desert people, man. Why would they leave doors out here? 'Cause the heat has fried their brains. Why are they isolated out here in the desert? 'Cause they don't like people."

"Even if it were just a psychotic person that put these up, they'd have to live near and have access to food and water."

"Yeah, our bodies are the food, and our blood is the water, and they'll have access to both of them once we're dead."

"If there was a crazy person here," I continue, "we'd outnumber them two to one."

"They hunt in packs, all armed to the teeth. You don't catch desert people slipping."

"Barry, plenty of people live in deserts. Not all of them are crazy. Where are you getting this information from?"

"Lots of places!! Have you seen—" Barry coughs for a few seconds. "Have you seen *The Hills Have Eyes*? That movie was crazy."

I start walking toward the door. "Well, if we see a scrappy looking shack, we'll scope it out before we go in."

Barry starts walking shortly behind me and continues rambling. "That's the thing, man. They find us before we find them."

I look around the flat plain and wave my hands in all directions in an exaggerated way. "I don't think anyone is going to sneak up on us in this place."

"You just don't get it, man," he says as he continues trailing behind me.

The second door is now about 100 yards away from us facing towards my 8 o'clock. It's different from the last door, looking much more modern. Rather than wood planks, this one looks like it's made from one solid piece of wood. It has the indented rectangular frames and a modern brass circular door knob. The wood isn't light gray like the last door; instead, it has an almost pure black color. The frame however, is the same color as the previous frame.

Barry's face is expressionless. A blank slate. I can't tell what mood he possesses. Suddenly, he decides to walk up in front of me. Perhaps he's eager to reach the door. His legs continue to drag in the sand, and he struggles to keep the lead. His hat still rests on his head with the fabric still sticking out from underneath it.

As soon as we find that town, we should head to the hospital. Actually, first, food and water. Then the hospital. But wait, hospitals have food and water, even if it is bad. I probably need to check into the hospital as well. I'm definitely dehydrated. I'm not sure what that does to your body, but I know it's not good.

Out of nowhere, I hear Barry scream. "Ayy, ayy, ayy, ayy! I see someone!"

I follow Barry's pointed finger toward the door and discover a person standing next to it. A woman. She is tan and wears a red head scarf that matches the skirt draped over her legs below her white, long-sleeved shirt. It doesn't appear that she has noticed us yet. Her attention is focused on the door.

On closer inspection, I realize that she isn't looking at the door itself, but rather, she's more focused on the frame above it, where the two letters had been engraved on the previous door. Maybe she knows something about the mysterious initials. More importantly, maybe she can direct us to where this town is. I start quickening my pace toward the woman, with Barry following quickly behind me.

When we're about 50 yards away, I yell "Hey! Excuse me. Can we talk to you?" At that moment, she grabs onto the knob. I look over at her in suspense to see if the door will open or refuse to budge like the previous one. I can just barely see her arm twisting the knob. She turns it so painfully slowly that I feel like the anticipation will kill me. She pulls the door toward her. It's open!

At this point, I'm sprinting toward her, stumbling as the thick sand clings to my feet. I don't look back to see if Barry is doing the same. Don't care. He can catch up later. I continue yelling. At about 20 yards out, I know she can definitely hear me. "Excuse me! Excuse me!"

She is either deaf or ignoring me. Either way, no amount of noise could deter her focus from the door, which is now completely swung open.

The door blocks my sight of whatever's inside except for a slight sliver of the top-left corner. In that sliver, all I see is blackness, but at the same time, it appears as if it's glowing.

The woman takes a step in. She's going inside the door! She can fit inside the door! One step in. Two steps in. She's now completely engulfed by the door, and I can't see her anymore. I'm ten feet away. I'm almost there. I see the door swinging back into its original position. It's about to shut. Don't shut, please, please don't shut! How is this door even moving? No one is touching it and no wind is pushing it ever so lightly.

I'm just about to touch the door when I hear it click back into its frame. My fingers are inches away from the knob when the entire door – frame and all – vanishes into thin air before me without leaving a trace.

I stand in utter shock, catching my breath and trying to contemplate what I just witnessed. I hear Barry slowly trudge up behind me. He is just as shocked as I am, with his left hand placed against his temple in confusion. He blurts out, "You want to tell me what the hell just happened? 'Cause I'ma be real, that's the weirdest thing that's ever happened to me in real life. And I'm stone cold sober." Barry pauses and waves his finger around, pointing in no particular direction. "And I've seen some weird stuff in my life. I told you there was weird people in the desert. Now do you believe me?"

Calmly, I reply, "Okay, let's evaluate the situation. The—"

"Screw your evaluation!" He interrupts. "Tell me what the hell just happened!"

"The first door had a latch that was jammed, so we couldn't open—"

"Nor we couldn't knock it down either," Barry adds.

"Yes," I continue. "With this new door, we saw someone go inside, and, once it closed behind them, it vanished into thin air."

"I think we're just going crazy. Or it's a desert mirage. Something like that."

"We both saw the exact same thing, though. And besides…" I trail off. That couldn't have been real. There's no way what I just witnessed had just happened. I know of desert mirages, but that was so vivid and distinct.

Maybe we're just hallucinating. From the heat, the lack of water, or both.

I look down and notice the footsteps the mysterious woman left behind. Completely unscathed, each step appears perfectly preserved from when she had left them. That was real. I don't know how to explain it, but that was real.

The footsteps lead off into the distance in the direction of the hills we had been following. I point toward the trail of footsteps. "Nevermind all this. Take a look at this. She

48

had to come from somewhere. Most likely a town."

Barry turns his attention to the ground where I'm pointing. "What if she came from nowhere like us? We'd just be walking further into our graves. Or worse, they could lead us back to a creepy old shack. Maybe she just escaped from that shack."

"The thought looms in the back of my head as well, but there's no other trails for us. Our travel is following a bunch of loose ends that have no connection to one another, but that is our best bet."

An unconfident half-smirk spreads across Barry's face. "I just feel at this point it's hopeless, man. I'm exhausted, chafing, burnt to hell, and for sure getting skin cancer, and have a busted shoulder now. I'm ready to just sit down and die. All this pain I have is a result of my stupid mistakes."

"Who says you're at fault for being here? Besides, we shouldn't stop now. What if the town's just around the corner?"

"What corner, man? All I see are footsteps that go off into nowhere."

"The range of hills it leads to are not too far off though. We can get to them in an hour if we're fast."

"Those aren't hills," he mumbles.

"What?"

"Those aren't hills," he yells louder. "Look closely, those are more god damn sand dunes."

I look more closely at what I previously assumed to be hills, realizing, to my dismay, that Barry is right. They are sand dunes. A long chain of them stretching out in either direction. "You're right," I say.

"She probably woke up like us in the middle of nowhere. Let's face it, that tree lied to us. There's no town here."

"Look to either side of us. If you notice, there doesn't appear to be any sign of life or civilization in either of these directions. Ahead of us, however, there's a chance of hope. Those footsteps are leading us to hope. Those imprints in the sand look like hope. No matter how slim it is, we just have to continue making our own imprints in the sand until we find where those came from."

"Alright, chill, chill," Barry says. "I get the point. You don't gotta keep nagging me about it. Let me just sit here for five minutes. I'm comfy and need to get sand out of my shoes."

Chapter 6

I notice that, as time passes, the footsteps we're following start to dissipate from the sand, even though there is still a complete lack of wind.   The shape of her shoe print in the sand remains perfect, but each imprint gets more shallow with time. If there was a logo laid below her shoes, you would still be able to identify it in the sand. Slowly but surely, any evidence of this woman passing through here is disappearing. Maybe our footprints are doing the same thing behind us. Back where we started, is it completely unscathed? Maybe someone is there looking around, noticing like I did that there is no sign of human interaction. Maybe that is why this desert's sand looks so pristine.

Soon enough, we'll be without a path to find where this woman came from. I don't think Barry has noticed the vanishing prints yet. I turn around to look at him looking straight at me. Confused, he asks, "What?"

"Nothing," I say back. "Just making sure that you are still back there." There's no benefit in telling Barry. It'll only stress him out more and would also throw in a sense of *I told you so* attitude at me. The former being more important.

We reach the wall of dunes. The footprints go up and over the top of the one in front of us. The woman's footsteps are almost gone at this point. Barry has to have noticed it by now too. I rush up the dune, hoping to see where the footsteps lead before they disappear completely. Ten feet from the top, and the footsteps are barely visible to the naked eye. I won't be able to see the footprints from a hundred feet away, let alone ten feet. I start running up the remainder of the dune with what little energy I have left.

Five feet from the top, and footsteps disappear completely. Nothing but smooth sand in front of me. My trail is now gone. "Damn it," I shout out, stopping in my tracks in defeat. I breathe heavily while staring at the ground, thinking. I reach for my cracked lips as if my hand could magically heal them.

Barry reaches me moments later and slowly treks past me with his shoulders slumped and his feet dragging. He stands at the top for a few seconds not saying a word. I expect to hear some sarcastic comment or, at the very least, for him to say *something*.

However, he remains completely silent. Confused, I look up to see him staring forward, his expression blank besides his gaping eyes.

"What?" I ask him. "What's on the other side?"

He extends his arm forward, pointing at whatever lies in front of him. All he blurts is a flat, atonal "Town."

Not believing him, I climb the short path and peer slowly over the hill. There it is. The town. The one I have been longing to see.

Barry starts sliding down the dune. "Well, what are you waiting for?"

I remind him of the wound on his head as I'm catching up to him. "Oh, yeah. I completely forgot about that," Barry says as he knocks on the back of his head. "A little scratch won't stop me."

I get a good look at the town when we reach the bottom. It seems old. It's clear the place has been around for a while. Quite big too. It seems the village is at least a square mile, possessing a labyrinth of roads. The buildings are square and made out of a white rock. Most being one story but some are two, with the roofs of the first levels acting as balconies for the second. The windows on the buildings are covered by thin cloths with no glass. To my knowledge, there's nowhere in the

United States that comes close to looking like this. The architecture looks Middle Eastern by design. Maybe African or reminiscent of certain parts of Asia.

There's a small well just outside of the town that's unoccupied with no one minding it. It's isolated with nothing around it. It has a small roof that shields it from the sun we can't see. We sprint over to it (or what counts as a sprint for us at this point). I reel the bucket from the well as quickly as I can, but it still isn't fast enough. I grab hold of the rusted metal bucket and press the edge against my lips. Thank god. I have never been so grateful for water. Even if it is unclean. I hand the pail over to Barry, who proceeds to unintentionally pour most of the remaining water all over himself before drinking the rest.

The well is the same white rocky material as the buildings around us. The same color as the small hills that are to the right and left of the town. There must not be too many resources around here.

I'm finally close enough to take notice of the interior of the town. Not the buildings, but what's in between them. I see two people standing in the street. The first is a hooded woman sweeping the dust in front of one of the structures; her skin was as dark as the absent night. Across the street from her is a pale old man in overalls, who sits in a chair, picking at his fingernails. Both of them appear to be minding their own business. Neither notices the other, nor do they see Barry and I. They appear locked in their own little world, ignoring all the ruckus we are making at their town well. Hopefully one of them speaks English.

I turn back to Barry as he lowers the rusted bucket back into the well. His Ohio State sweatshirt is entirely soaked. I walk up to the man in overalls and ask him, "Hi, do you speak English? We're trying to find the hospital."

Without looking up from his fingernails, the man responds coldly in a language I don't know. "Nemluvím anglicky"

"Ummm, alright," I say to myself.

Barry comes up behind me and asks, "Yo, what's going on?"

"I just asked him where the hospital is, but I don't believe he speaks English."

"Oh, I got this. You ever play charades? I can do this."

"Barry I don't think—"

"Here, watch this." Barry walks up to the man in overalls, who is in the act of lighting a cigarette. Barry says "hey" in an attempt to get the man's attention before pointing at his head and acting out our travels with his body movements.

The man's only movement is his hand moving to his mouth to puff his cigarette. He sends an icy stare to Barry. He exhales the smoke from his cigarette and says, "jsi mrtvý," as he points down one of the roads.

"Thank you," I tell the man. Barry presses his hands together and bows to him.

"I told you, I could do my magic," Barry says cockily.

We walk several blocks down the road and see no sign of the hospital. Just houses and houses. There aren't too many people out on the street. Maybe everyone is inside, hiding from the heat. As we walk, I notice that there aren't really any smells in the air here. I don't know, I guess I was assuming I would smell spices from food being cooked in these homes. All I smell is the dirt path we walk on. Every drag of our feet kicks up a little bit of dust. Our feet scraping the dirt is the loudest sound here. Nothing else seems to be competing with it.

We see a blond man sitting down and leaning against the wall of one of the houses. He is wearing a gray army uniform covered with holes on his chest. He looks rather bored, as if he yearns for any form of entertainment. I walk up to him with Barry right behind me.

I try to get his attention. "Excuse me."

The man is startled by my presence and jumps a little when he hears my voice. He looks up at us quickly, his eyes wide in surprise.

"Do you speak English?" I ask.

He shakes his head.

Barry brushes past me and asks, "Tu parles français?"

The man holds up his pointer finger and thumb in a gesture to tell us he speaks a little bit.

"Bon bon. Où est l'hôpital?" Barry asks the man.

The man gives us a big grin and starts laughing hysterically. He points to the array of holes adorning the front of his uniform.

Barry looks at me to see if I am just as confused as him. The man notices we are not amused, stops chuckling, fixes his posture, and points down the road.

"Could you ask him where we are?" I tell Barry.

"Où sommes-nous?"

"Dans une ville" he says in a thick accent I can't place.

"What did he say?" I ask Barry.

"He says we're in a town."

The man begins laughing to himself again, this time more reserved.

Barry says "Merci" to the man as we head the way he pointed.

From behind us, I hear the man say "Au revoir" with one last chuckle.

Walking through this town just raises more questions. We don't come across too many people, and the ones we do encounter are quite diverse. All kinds of different skin tones and clothing, with each person seeming to speak a different language. The age range is quite wide as well, though I don't see many kids.

We end up in the town square with a fountain in the center surrounded by a number of people occupied with various tasks. There is a woman dressed like a Vietnamese rice farmer taking a nap on a bench with her hat blocking the sun. There's a man sitting next to her, wearing an African-style Zebra-stripe tunic and staring forward at nothing specific; he looks as if he's just waiting out the day. Opposite side of the fountain is a pale young woman wearing a Gucci sweater chatting with an older man in a zhongshan suit. Their conversation seems lighthearted, as I notice the woman smiling and the older man laughing a few times.

That's when my attention is directed to the center of the plaza, where a man stands motionless next to the fountain, staring at his own reflection in the water. He is a bigger man who is wearing jeans and a plain white T-shirt. Leaving Barry to explore on his own, I walk up to the man at the fountain and ask, "Excuse me, sir. Do you speak English?"

With a short pause, he responds "Yes" in a thick Southern accent.

"Thank goodness. We're trying to find the hospital. Do you happen to know where it is?"

He looks me up and down, taking in my full profile.

"Your attire do be fancy for a place like this."

His response catches me off guard, and I pause momentarily. "Excuse me?" I respond.

"But you do look like you've been beat all to hell, mister."

"Look. I don't have time for casual chit-chat. My friend needs to see a doctor."

"I don't mean no offense, stranger. There goes my blabber mouth causing all sorts of trouble again. You folks must be new here, huh?"

"Yeah, we just came into town actually, but about the doc—"

The man cuts me off. "Well, I'd tell you the whole story, but I've grown rather tired and don't have the energy to tell such a tale. However, I can point you in the right direction." The man points across the town square. "See that building with the *i* on the front of it?"

The building he points at possesses nothing except for a simple door with a lowercase *i* engraved above it. "Yes," I answer. "Is that the hos—"

"All the information you need will be right inside there," he interrupts.

"Thank you for the assistance."

"It ain't no sweat. Say, do you happen to have a cigarette? I smoked my last one earlier."

I shake my head.

"Aww, shucks. If you come across some, don't be afraid to bum some to your new pal, Hank."

"Will do," I say while walking away.

I head back to Barry, who is laying on a small patch of grass by the fountain. I kick his side a little to wake him up. He looks up toward me.

"I talked to a man," I explain. "He told me to head to that building."

Barry lazily looks over at the building. "That doesn't look too much like a hospital," he says as he slowly gets up.

"Well, beggars can't be choosers."

We approach the entrance to the mysterious *i* building. The door is in pristine condition, as if it was installed yesterday. Gray door attached to a gray frame. No sign of wear and tear. The wood is not rotten and dry from the dreadful heat, and there doesn't seem to be a single speck of dirt or dust on it.

The door knob looks like it was polished only mere moments before we walked up. No streaks of oil or fingerprints from a human hand. An intense shine to it. I look around at other doors on the surrounding buildings and see they don't share the same fate.

I grab the handle and notice it's not scorching hot to the touch from being in the sun. I open the door, and a breeze of cool air ambushes me.

"Oh, thank god," I hear Barry say behind me.

We enter the room and see it almost completely bare, except for a desk situated behind a glass barrier. All the walls, the ceiling, and the floor were the same shade of white. A man sits behind the desk, wearing what looks like mid gray nurse's scrubs. He looks no older than 30. He is tapping his pencil against the desk, clearly bored. He notices us when Barry shuts the door behind me. The man straightens his posture in a quick manner. As we reach the glass barrier that separates us, he asks, "How can I help you gentlemen?"

"Hello," I say. "We were looking for a doctor, and we were told to come here."

The man attempts to hide a smirk. "Would you guys like a drink? I got everything from coffee to beer to even milkshakes."

"Yeah, can I get a whiskey sour with Tullamore Dew?" Barry quickly responds.

The man gives us a wink and points finger guns at Barry. "You got it. And for you?"

"Just water, please."

"Sure thing," the man responds.

He heads to a door on our right and swings it open toward us, blocking our view of the room as he enters. He comes back with a glass of water in one hand and a yellow drink in a short glass in the other. He slips them through a metal slot on the barrier like a late night gas station attendant.

"Yeah, it's always better to hear the news when you have a nice cold beverage in your hand. Especially in these parts."

"What news?"

"To put it bluntly, you're dead."

I stop sipping my water. "What?" I scoff at the man.

Barry chuckles a bit. "Haha, alright, Chief, where's the camera crew? I ain't falling for this one." He takes a sip from his drink. "God damn, this is the best whiskey sour I've ever had. Props to you."

"I know it is," the man says before continuing in a calm and collected manner. "People always deny it at first. One time, some guy started calling me obscene names and tried breaking the glass barrier when he heard the news." He pauses to see the reactions on our faces. "Alright. I see you two still aren't convinced. I'm guessing you didn't die in a hospital bed surrounded by your family?" He indicates a screen on the desk and says, "Look, your profiles are already pulled up. James Davis and Barry Ross."

"How do you know our names?" I ask, confused. "I didn't even know Barry's last name."

"I didn't," the man quickly responds. "The system did. I'm just reading the words from off the screen. Don't shoot the messenger." He jokingly holds up his hands in surrender.

Barry looks over to me. "This is a prank. Don't fall for it." He begins scanning all around the room in an attempt to find a camera. "Which one of my friends set me up in this?"

"Look," the man responds in a slightly impatient tone. "I've done this many, many times. Not lately, though." The man continues talking as his eyes wander around the room. "They've started sending fewer and fewer people to these parts. Not sure why, though. You two are the first clients I've had in weeks. Good thing, I guess. One time, a man came in here crawling saying he had been in the desert for 'weeks.'" He turns his attention back over to us. "Oh, please forgive me. I'm rambling again. Let's start with you, Mr. Davis." He begins reading off the screen in front of him. "Died January 28th, 2020, at 7:55 a.m. local time." I look down at my watch as he continues. "Cause of death: brain aneurysm. A bit of a boring way to go out, I would say, but nonetheless painless. Or so I'm assuming. I don't really know."

I put my finger on my temple instinctively, as if it would bring additional information to this news.

"Now let's take a look at Mr. Ross," the man continues. "Died January 27th at 11:58 p.m. local time. Cause of death: blunt force trauma to the head." Barry rubs the back of his head as he listens.

I remain skeptical, unsure of what to believe. No way could this be a prank show. Drop us off in the desert without our knowing so we can march to the point of death? A show like that would result in a ridiculous amount of lawsuits before they could even finish shooting the first season.

There's no way we're dead. We're both conscious. I rub the rough fabric on the side of my coat. Bits of sand fall into my palm, and I rub them in between my finger and thumb. This all feels very real.

The man looks up from his screen back towards us. "Alright, I see you two still aren't convinced one bit. Don't want to be too gullible, but, at the same time can't live your life in suspicion. Would you like to see a video of your death? I've got them pulled up right here."

"Alright, Mr. Man. Show me the money," Barry says.

"Okay, Mr. Ross. Have—"

"Please, just call me Barry," Barry quickly interjects.

"Okay, Barry. Have a look here."

The man pulls up an additional screen from below his desk and presses it up against the glass barrier. On the screen, Barry stands on a balcony of a house with a few other people late at night. There's music playing in the background. All of them are holding red Solo cups as they talk and laugh. None of them seems to have an ounce of sobriety in them.

"Wait, wait, wait. You guys stalking me or something? How'd you get this footage?" Barry's voice is equal parts confused and concerned.

"Where is this from?" I ask Barry.

"That was that rager at Ohio State from the other night."

The man behind the glass pauses the video and lets out a sigh. "Gentlemen, I must ask that there be no more interruptions, please. And, to assure you, no one in my department was stalking you. We've obtained these through the archives."

Barry in a hostile tone, says, "What archives?"

The man behind the glass raises his palm to us . "I am not allowed to say anymore. Please, can we continue with this?"

Barry and I stand silent.

"Excellent."

The video continues to play. Barry stands in a circle of people, but he doesn't seem focused on the conversation at hand. Rather, he just stares into his red Solo cup. He looks as if he is in an almost trance-like state, lost in deep thought. The group erupts into laughter, snapping Barry out of it. He looks up to see a few of them staring at him. He does a fake laugh and asks, "What's up? What'd I miss?"

A woman wearing banana earrings responds, "What's up? You're quiet over there, Barry. Was my joke not funny to you?

"No, it's not that. I was just thinking."

"Thinking about what? What's going on in that little head of yours?" Her smile on her face disappears and her eyes show concern. "Are you thinking about Mabel again?"

Barry smirks and waves off the answer with his hand. He pauses for a second and then runs toward the balcony's thin railing, stumbling over himself on the way there. "Yo, watch me walk across this railing."

The woman with banana earrings says, "Barry I don't think that's a good—"

"Aww, Jamie you're no fun." Barry grabs the railing, seemingly evaluating its strength. "Where's your wild side?" Barry climbs on top of the railing, rises into a standing position, and balances with his arms spread wide.

A man in the group calls out, "Yeah, Barry, Jamie is right. Get down. I don't think that railing is able to hold your—"

The sound of wood snapping and a woman shrieking interrupts everything. Barry falls from the second-story balcony, landing head first on a rock with a loud thud, followed by haunting stillness. A crowd slowly forms there silently, each of them hoping the person next to them knows what to do.

"That's some pretty gruesome stuff right there," says the man behind the glass. "Of course, I've seen far worse stuff before. Not to brag."

Barry is silent. His expression is flat. I try to say something, but every sentence I create in my mind is half built.

The man behind the glass looks toward me and aims his hand toward the screen. "What about you, Mr. Davis? Would you like to go next? Although, I must warn you, it's probably not as entertaining as Barry's."

I shake my head. "No, I don't think that is necessary."

The man puts the screen away and leans back in his chair. "Looks like I finally convinced the both of you."

After a short moment of silence, I ask, "So what is this place? Heaven, hell, pur—"

"I am not allowed to disclose that information," the man quickly responds.

"So this is it. We are dead. Is this the end of the line?" I ask.

"I can't disclose any more information," the man repeats. "I'm already on two strikes from previous cases." He gives off a light laugh. "Huh, must be why they're sending fewer individuals my way, actually. Anyway, I'd ask the locals. They can relay more information to you than I can."

"Thanks," I say, my voice monotone and devoid of inflection.

We start heading toward the door when the man yells, "Oh! Almost forgot." We turn around and see him ruffling through supplies inside his desk. "C'mon, I know I had a few more in here. Aha! Here we go." The man slides a few small pieces of paper through the slot. "Here's some drink tickets for your troubles. You can redeem them over at the The Deep Dive a few blocks away. I heard they make the drinks strong there."

Barry mumbles "Thanks," making no effort to hide his ungrateful attitude.

"If you want, I can take them back."

Barry retracts the drink tickets into his chest. "No, no. We're good."

"Thank you for the information and time uh - what's your name?" I ask. "I never caught it."

"No thanks necessary. It's my job. Can't disclose my name but the locals call me Gary for some reason."

Chapter 7

With nowhere else to go, we leave to find The Deep Dive. Barry for drinks, myself for answers. Me and Barry don't say anything to each other as we walk. I don't really know what to say to him, and I'm sure he feels the same. Only a few blocks away from the *i* building, we come upon the bar.

The moldy and unkept front door, with one loose hinge and the second one close to falling off, seems barely attached to its frame. One hard swing would be enough for it to fall off completely.

A man stands next to the door, dressed in all black and smoking a cigarette. He is tall and intimidating with sunglasses hiding where he looks. We wait for him to say something as we walk by, but he remains as still and quiet as a statue. When we finally reach for the door, the man breaks his silence. "You two new?" he asks in a deep voice.

"How could you tell?" I ask.

He points to the drink tickets that Barry is gripping in his hand. He goes back to smoking his cigarette and puts his attention elsewhere, not seeming to care if I have a response for him.

We open the door and a burst of cigarette smoke greets us. The smell is a mix of cigarettes, dirt, and stagnant air. This place has to be the seediest bar I've ever been to. A wide variety of individuals occupy the seats inside here, including an Asian man in a three-piece suit who is clearly hitting on a white woman wearing a leather jacket and fishnets. At one table, there is a group of men playing cards; one of them looks like the stereotypical cowboy while another wears traditional Native American attire.

"Hey there, friend." A familiar voice floats in our direction.

I look to my right and notice Hank walking up to us with a smudged glass of beer in his hand.

"Oh, hello. Good to see you again," I respond.

"Thought I'd find you here." He takes a drink. "They always send the shinies here. By the drink tickets in your hand, I'd say Gary gave you the news."

"He did but left out a lot of details about anything," I say.

"Those bureaucrats, am I right? Don't worry, old Hank can help you out." A sly grin spreads across his face. "For a price, that is."

"Oh, Hank, I don't have any mo—"

"Those drink tickets in your hand there," he interrupts. "One of those suckers can be redeemed for a pack of stoges. I say the information I gave earlier and the info I'm about to give is definitely worth a pack for your pal Hank."

I grab one from Barry's palm and hand it to him.

"Much obliged. I'll meet you over there at that table," he says as he points to an empty table off in a dark corner of the bar.

"I'm going to get a drink, man. Do you want one?" Barry asks me.

"Just get me water."

"Just water? Ight, I guess."

I wait at the table in the corner, watching Barry talk with the bartender and Hank converse with a table of people all smoking cigarettes. I tilt my head back and close my eyes for a second.

So I'm dead. I wonder how my parents felt. What were their reactions when they found out? What about my wife? I wonder if she even shed a tear for me. What was the funeral like? Have they even had it yet?

I already know the world is going just fine without me. Everyone is just going on as if I never existed. My boss is already looking for someone to fill my position. My wife is carrying on with her day. My dad's probably on the couch watching TV while my mother is going to her yoga classes like their normal schedules. Thanksgiving dinner will have one less seat filled. A seat that will be forgotten over time. Left in the corner, collecting dust until it is ultimately thrown out as there's no longer a use for it. Gone but forgotten.

"Here you go, Chief." Barry's voice breaks me out of my thoughts. He hands me a glass of water.

"Thank you," I respond with a slight hesitation. I notice all the smudges and stains on the glass and how the water has a grayish tint to it. On closer inspection, I spot a piece of chipped glass just swimming along inside the water. Well it can't kill me I guess.

In the *i* building, the water was crystal clear, with no imperfections or dirt on the glass. It was the perfect amount of cold. Not freezing but not room temperature either. I really took that water for granted. At the time, I was more focused on the news at hand and wasn't paying attention to how good that water truly was.

I fish out the chipped piece of glass and down the drink in one gulp despite my body telling me not to. I try to avoid the taste touching my tongue, but alas, I can't avoid the stale taste of dirt. It is warmer than I imagined it to be. They probably leave the water barrel outside in the sun to make space for the more prized inventory here. I look around and, sure enough, no one else here is drinking water. The bartender probably gave Barry a weird look when he asked for it.

Barry looks at the charade of contorted facial expressions I've been making and laughs at my expense. "Having trouble keeping it down? It's only water. Watch a pro drink." He sips from his drink and almost spits it out when it comes into contact with his tongue. With great effort, he swallows it, gulping like there's a rock going down his throat. "I don't think that was real whiskey," he mutters.

"I don't think we can be picky around here." All the other patrons drink what's in their glasses with no hesitation. "I'm assuming we'll just have to take what we get."

Barry sets his glass back down on the table. "So what do you think there's to do around here besides drinking, 'cause I'm not getting much enjoyment from this glass."

"Well, there's sweating, but I think we've both had our fill of that."

"If there wasn't alcohol, I'd figure this place was hell for sure," Barrys says.

Barry stares at the "alcohol" left in his glass. I can tell he is deep in thought. He was looking at his drink the same way he was in the video.

"So who's Mabel?" I ask Barry.

Barry lets out a long sigh. Without looking up from his drink, he begins speaking. "Remember when I told you I moved to Ohio with my family?"

"Yeah."

"I lied. I got no family he— there. I came there by myself. In California, I was dating this girl named Mabel. We've been dating for years. I knew she was the one."

His expression and voice becomes more excited as he talks. "Her laugh was amazing. Her smile was delicate and fragile. Her sense of humor was god-tier. When I woke up next to her, it made my day."

Barry takes a long pause followed by a big swig of his drink. "That all fell apart, though," he says, his face once again draining of any expression. "We split, and I couldn't handle being without her. Every time I went somewhere familiar, I would see the memories we made there together. I couldn't handle that. I caught a plane that took me across the country. No warning to my family or pals. Got off. Started a new life. Worked in a deli during the days. Partied throughout the night. I guess I was walking down a path of self-destruction to forget her. I guess that path brought me here."

"Why did your relationship with her end?"

Barry slams his glass aggressively on the table. A few people at the surrounding tables turn their heads in our direction. In an aggressive tone, he barks, "It doesn't matter how it ended. What matters is that it ended. The outcome is the same, so what's the point? It's in the past so I have to learn to move on."

He looks around the bar. The people at the other tables turn away. "Especially now in this situation," he adds quietly.

"I'm sorry. I didn't mean to agitate you," I say.

Barry mumbles a few words under his breath before he finishes the rest of his drink. He sits there in silence for a few seconds, studying the splintered table.

"So how did you meet your wife?" he casually asks.

"I don't recall mentioning I had a wife to you."

"Nah, but your ring did," Barry says, pointing at my finger.

"Well. I was dating this girl. We met in college. She had a different major from me, but we saw each other around. One day, I saw her lying alone on a patch of grass and asked her out, and she said yes. When I first introduced her to my parents, they disapproved of her. Said she wasn't the 'right material for me,' quote unquote."

"I feel you." Barry nods slowly. "One time, I brought home this girl from a party, and my mom made me sleep outside for a week."

"Alright. Anyways, my parents eventually pressured me to break up with her by threatening to remove their contribution to my tuition and not allow me to move back home."

"That's crazy," Barry says with his mouth full of ice. "So did you break up with her?"

"Yes. It was the hardest thing I had to do in my life."

"How did she take it?" Barry asks between bites of ice.

"Not well. I broke her heart and mine simultaneously. Haven't talked to her since that day. I told my parents, and they were ecstatic. Right after, they introduced me to a girl they felt was more suited for me. We didn't really click with each other, but we tried faking it and making the best of it for a while. That eventually caught up though. Long story short, I ended up marrying a woman who has no love towards me."

"Man. You should've just told your parents to screw off. That's what I would've done."

"I wish I could. I just didn't have the confidence to stand up to my parents. The confidence in myself. If the same situation happened today, would I make a different decision than before?"

"Have you ever tried finding the girl from college?" Barry asks.

"Once or twice. I couldn't locate her anywhere on social media. Must've married someone and changed her surname. Besides, even if I did find her, would she even want to hear from me? After all the heartbreak I've caused her, she must think I'm heartless."

Seemingly at a loss for words, Barry nods his head. We sit in silence for a few seconds, each waiting for the other to speak.

Barry finally says, "Well, I guess there's no reason to cry about all this now. I'm sure everyone else here has their demons and regrets as well."

Staying silent, I give him a slight nod in agreement.

"Hey, maybe they'll eventually end up here though," Barry says. "We can go look for our ex-broads in around 40 to 60 years."

"I can't imagine residing in this place for 60 years," I say back.

"Well, I guess we better learn to, 'cause I'm looking around and see some very old clothing here. Who knows, maybe time flows differently here."

"I haven't seen any Neanderthals yet," I comment.

"Wait," Barry blurts out. "I wonder if my grandma is somewhere nearby. She hit the can about four years ago. Do you think this whole place is like a desert? Can't imagine her walking through those dunes with her knee replacement."

"Oh, trust me, there are many great parts to this land here," Hank says, heading toward us with a lit cigarette in his mouth. "You just happened to end up in a not-so-purdy part." He takes a seat in one of the empty chairs between me and Barry.

"'Bout time you joined us," says Barry.

"Sorry, mister. Didn't realize you was in a hurry. Have an important meeting to attend to? Pick up yer daughter from soccer practice?"

Barry is silent.

"Now I don't know if you two folks picked up on the environment here yet, but people 'round here aren't in too big of a hurry. We're dead!" Hank shouts ecstatically. "We got all the time in the world to get everything we want done and then some."

"So this is it?" I ask.

"Is that what those folks in that building are saying now?"

"They didn't tell us anything," Barry chimes in.

"The all-knowing sure don't like sharing their all-knowing knowledge." Hank grabs another cigarette and lights it, flicking the ash on the floor at his feet. I look down at the floor and notice that every table has a small mound of cigarette ash beneath it.

Hank continues. "So this here place isn't the *afterlife* afterlife. It's like some sort of waiting room. Some people refer to it as 'limbo.' Some people call it 'purgatory.' Both similar concepts but both are not where we are. Doesn't matter."

Barry interrupts. "So, like, we're here until a higher power says we can leave? Just serving like a sentence 'til we can go to Heaven?"

"No. Now, if I may finish, basically you have to be ready to leave this here place." He takes another puff and coughs a little bit.

"I'm ready to leave this place," I say jokingly.

"Doesn't work like that, unfortunately. Now when you guys were out there, did y'all stumble across some doors attached to a frame and nothing else?"

"Yeah, we've stumbled into two of them out in the desert. A woman stepped inside one and disappeared," I mention quickly, eager to finally learn more about the strange doorways.

"Those doors are like personal portals out of this place. Only the person they're designed for are able to open them. Where they go? No one knows except for the people behind the glass, and they're not too keen on giving out that information. Could take you to Heaven. Maybe Hell. Heck, for all we know, it could even send you to be reincarnated. But everyone who's stepped into one of those doors has never returned.

"Man, that's some high stakes gambling right there," Barry says, his mouth full of ice.

"How do we find our door?" I ask.

Hank chuckles. "That's the thing. You don't. The door finds you. It's at the exact spot when you're ready to move on. Right now, it's somewhere out there, just waiting. It's been here since the second you arrived."

"I didn't see any of these doors inside this town," I mention.

"Are you really that surprised?" he asks, laughing as he looks around the bar. "These people are pretty keen on staying here."

"Hank. Let me ask you. What's the average time people spend here?"

"Now there for certain is no average here. A lot of people find their door within a day of arriving here, others weeks, months, years, decades, centuries. I've met someone that proclaims they came here before Jesus Christ was born." Hank takes another puff of his cigarette. "That guy sure was an asshole. Anyways, people who end up in these parts though have a tendency to stay quite a bit longer. With the dunes just to the south, this area has been coined the term, 'The Sea of Lost Souls'. Not too many people who come to these parts leave. At least, not in a hurry that is."

"Do you have any plans of ditching this place and getting in your door or whatever?" asks Barry.

"My focus isn't on doors. My focus is here. Who else is going to smoke all these cigarettes, drink all these drinks, and gamble all these chips? I'm having a blast!"

"Hell yeah to that," Barry says, forcing a fistbump from Hank.

"How did you die?" I ask Hank.

"People here don't really talk about that stuff," Hank says swiftly.

"Oh, okay. Well, thank you for all this information," I tell Hank.

Hank shakes the cigarette pack in his hand. "Thank you for the compensation, friend. If you need any more info, you know the place and the price."

As I'm about to leave the table, a man bursts through the door of the bar in an over exaggerated way to get everyone's attention. He possesses a thin beard and a cocky smile. The man screams across the bar, making sure every patron notices his presence. "Good morrow! I see ye gents started thy festivities without me."

Everyone in the bar – Hank included – picks up a glass and holds it in the air. In unison, they shout "Huzzah!" back to the man. The man turns his attention to our table – more specifically, to me and Barry, the only two who haven't raised their glasses. The cocky smile turns into a confused and offended look. He looks away and turns his attention to the bar keep.

"Who is that?" I ask Hank.

"That guy there is the mayor of this town. The head honcho in these parts. Mayor Andrew Clark."

"You guys have a mayor here?" asks Barry.

"Well, sure. We have to have some order around here. In this town's constitution, the oldest person that resides here automatically becomes mayor. No one cares enough to go out and vote here, so they just set it up this way to be easier."

"How can you tell if they are the oldest?" I asked Hank.

"Honestly, we really don't care. Mayors here don't really have much authority. All power comes from those fellers behind the glass. The mayor is more of a figurehead. A mascot, as they say."

"How long has he been mayor here?" I ask.

"Well, he's been mayor since I've shown up to this town, but I hear the mayor before him was someone named Fatima."

"O, Fatima, a muddy-mettled and fain mistris," a voice says towards our table. "Pain in thy breeches, 'tis no matter the codpiece. That's all ye gents must know'st that wench."

We all turn to see the man who possesses that voice is the one in colorful and vibrant attire, staring down at us with a glass of beer in his hand. He's wearing a top that is bright pink. His pants, also pink, reach down to his shins, where they meet his teal socks. His cape, also teal, seems to flow elegantly, even with the absence of wind.

"Andrew, pleasure to see you again," Hank says. "What brings you to our table?"

"I would not have come hither if not to see how ye gents don't salute thy mayor," Andrew says with annoyance in his voice. "Art thou treacherous, discontented villains Hank? Shall I punish all three of thee?"

"Don't mind them, friend," Hank responds. "They just showed up into town within the last hour. I'm showing them the ropes as we speak." Hank hands the man a cigarette to ease the situation.

The man grabs the cigarette and an additional one from the pack in Hank's other hand. He grabs a lighter out of his pocket as he speaks. Without breaking eye contact with us, he says "Ye speak of showing these gents the ropes, but yet they know not proper manners here."

Hank tugs the collar of his shirt. "Well I— I was just getting to that."

The mayor stands there in silence for a second before letting out a big, hearty laugh. "At ease, gents! I am only tugging thy chains. A good laugh is all."

The man grabs the empty seat at our table across from Hank. He takes a long puff from his cigarette. "Hank, thy cigarettes be terrible." He leans back in his old, decrepit chair that looks like it's about to collapse under its own weight and rests his legs on the worn table. The chair creaks with every slight movement he makes. "Thus, in this time of meeting, who have we here? Possess mine name of Andrew Clark as well as hold title of mayor to this village. Been so for many moons. Pray, what is your origin?"

Barry says, "Ohio. And he's from New York. What about you, Chief?"

Andrew's brow furrows in concern. "Chief? As mayor, chief I am indeed, yet I do wonder if I inspire mis*chief*?" His tone calms. "It doesn't matter where I reside from acquaintances. Of import 'tis that I am the oldest in these parts, and that will not be changing."

The man chugs the remainder of his drink   while Hank begins lighting another cigarette.

"Now, for my life, has Hank told thee about the 'party mansion' in which I stay?"

Barry's interest is piqued, and he shakes his head in excitement. "Party mansion?"

"O, heavens, Hank. I thought thou were telling thee about essentials."

Hank shrugs his shoulders. "I told them what I thought the essentials would be for them. The doors. The—"

Andrew holds up a finger, silencing Hank. "You mustn't address matters such as 'doors' with new guests. We don't hinder such objects to thou's town. Does thou want thy guests leaving so soon?"

He turns his attention from Hank to me and Barry. "Well, ye folks must attend. Come thither to my place. The only place in the region where thou can celebrate! Hank, thou art welcome to accompany as well."

"I will have to pass up on your offer, Mister Mayor. There are some cards at that table with my name on them. Maybe I'll join up when my luck dries up."

"Thine loss."

Chapter 8

Andrew Clark brought us back to his house that he self-proclaims as his mansion. Although it would not be considered a mansion by today's standards, it definitely boasts a larger square footage than the rest of the residential buildings in town. I noticed a garden of cacti in the entryway of the house. Inside, there are multiple bathrooms, an open kitchen, multiple bedrooms, and a couple living rooms.

As we walk through the house (which anyone is allowed to enter as long as they're 'chill'), the mayor tells us more about the town. The people here are a wide variety. Different languages. Different cultures. People here either don't really understand or relate to each other. But it doesn't matter to them. People here don't want to listen. They want to forget. Forget what? Forget that they're here? Forget why they're here? Forget about the troubles they have? Drown their sorrows in alcohol or any other substance they can get their hands on?

Rather than moving on and finding their door, they choose to stay. Why do they choose to stay? Did they have unfinished business here or in the living world? Maybe they have just become too comfortable in this holding state and don't know how to change. Are they searching for a loved one? Searching for answers? In the mayor's "party mansion," however, the only thing people are searching for is the bottom of the bottle. Only thing here are lost souls. But, at the same time, am I a lost soul myself.

I have never been found or found myself – found who I truly was or truly could have been. I couldn't figure myself out when I was alive. Can I figure myself out here? In this town? Right now, it's in my hands on what I decide. Do I let this house consume my soul like it has consumed the many other souls rotting away here?

Barry has acclimated himself to the lifestyle of this house almost immediately. However, I'm sure this was quite near the lifestyle he was living when he was alive. Right now, he's in the kitchen area with a woman in baggy jeans and a psychedelic shirt. The lively music from a nearby record player prevents me from hearing their words, but it doesn't matter what they are talking about anyway. It's nonsense. Whatever they say won't project them further. Whatever they say won't get them out of this situation. We are stagnant.

In this place, we are all stagnant. No progress is made. This place is not for the sober mind. The conversations people have here are forgotten in hours, if not seconds. They could meet again, have the same conversations as before not knowing the loop they are following. Everyone will eventually run out of stories to tell. I doubt any new stories are created here. Maybe they do know that these stories are being retold. Maybe they only repeat them just to have something to converse about. Something to bury the noises of their head. Something to oppress the silence they themselves might be afraid of.

As Barry talks to the woman with the baggy jeans, I take a seat on a couch in one of the living rooms. There are two people on the couch with me. To one side of me is a frail old Asian man who has remained silent smoking something out of his long pipe. On the other side is a darker-toned obese man. He is drinking and keeps trying to talk to me in a language which I don't understand. I try telling him I don't speak his language multiple times, but, at this point, I feel he's more just speaking to himself and using me as an audience.

Andrew enters the room and is just starting to make his rounds and greet his guests when he spots me on the couch. He interrupts his current conversation and walks straight toward me.

"Sir James. I don't see anything in thy hand, nor a smile on thy pale face. Is anything amiss?"

"Nothing, really. I'm just not thirsty is all."

"Nonsense. Nonsense. Come hither at my 'refrigerator' filled with plenty of ale."

"Alright," I say reluctantly.

I get up and follow Andrew to the kitchen. We pass by Barry, who proceeds to give me a nod and grin while still talking to the girl. Andrew Clark opens his fridge to reveal that it is filled with nothing but countless varieties of alcohol and a single loaf of bread. "Try this ale out. I don't understand the tongue written on the side of the bottle, but it does the job. Even if it has an attitude to it."

He hands me a black bottle with a bronze label that has Asian characters on it. "Thank you. I appreciate it," I tell him.

"Of course!" he says explosively. "A mayor is no host, and a host would certainly never be mayor if he does not attend to his guest's needs."

"So where did this beer come from?" I ask sarcastically. "Does beer randomly pop up here once someone drinks it in the living world?"

Andrew, not catching on to my stupid joke, gives me a funny look. "Nay," he responds. "Was crafted in a brewery in the next village o'er. We trade our livestock for ale."

"Interesting" is all I respond.

Andrew gives a half hearted look around and says "Now, I'll wander on by again once thee finishes thine ale. Adieu."

I raise my beer and let out a small "Huzzah" to Andrew.

He laughs. "I knew not to take thee for a fool!" He slaps my shoulder light heartedly and leaves the kitchen. I see him grab a smoke from a man in the other room and begin chatting with them. Again, I am left alone in a sea of people. I take a sip of the beer Andrew handed me. The taste was bitter and appalling. I almost spat it out as soon as it touched my tongue.

"Tastes like shit, yeah?"

I turn around and see a tall blonde woman. Her dress is blue with white polka dots. The pointed collar of an undershirt stuck out from her dress.

"That's everyone's first reaction to that beer," she says.

"I wish I could've received a warning before drinking it," I respond.

"They gave you one," she says as she points at the bottle. "You just can't read it."

"You have a unique accent. Where are you from?" I ask.

With a carefree smile, she responds, "Soviet Ukraine. Been here while."

I laugh. "I can tell. I'm surprised you can speak English."

"Mayor Andrew taught me. Did thou just arrive?"

"Yeah, I just got here. I'm from New York."

"Ohhhh, the Big Apple," she says, waving her hands around in mock awe. "Always wanted to go."

I chuckle. "It's not as good as people say. It's dirty and full of terrible people."

"Sounds like Ukraine village. I'll fit right in," she responds, a grin teasing the corner of her mouth.

We both laugh, and I ask her name.

"Olga," she responds.

I tell her my name, and we keep talking. She is young – or *was* young. She looks no older than 30. She grabs a bottle of tequila from the table next to us. When she raises the bottle to her mouth, her sleeve falls down her arm, revealing nothing but skin and bones. There isn't a muscle or ounce of fat on her entire arm. She notices me staring and swiftly puts the bottle down and fixes her sleeve.

"Oh," she says self-consciously. "Don't mind that. No matter how much thou eats or drinks, thou remain the same weight as when thou died."

"I'm sorry. I didn't mean to stare."

"It's no trouble," she says as she picks up the tequila bottle again, this time holding on to her sleeve as she drinks. She puts the bottle down and says "There sex party happening in back room in 10 minutes. Care to join?"

I wave my hand with my wedding ring on it. "No, thank you. I'll politely decline."

"'Til death do us part, no?"

I wave goodbye and head back to the living room. The spot on the couch has been claimed by someone else, so I kind of just stand in the corner for a bit, pretending to drink the bitter beer I was given.

I have no idea what I'm doing here. I don't belong here. In fact, I don't belong in any part of this place. If I leave this house, where will I end up? On the side of the road, just waiting. Waiting like the rest of these people in the village. Whether they know it or not, they are all just waiting. Waiting for what? Waiting for the inevitable? Waiting for nothing? Just trying to prevent it for as long as possible.

I could find an apartment or house here. A lot of the buildings seem abandoned. I'd pay for it with whatever currency they have here, which I'd earn by working whatever jobs they have here. I don't think there's high demand for bankers. Could be a sheep herder. But then again, every second I work, every second I relax in my new home, I'll still be thinking and wondering answers. Knowing this place isn't the final stop. Merely only a waiting room. What is on the other side of that door? I need a conclusion. I need to know. I can't just wait here, letting my mind wander, coming to conclusions, and replacing those conclusions with new conclusions.

I don't deserve a conclusion, though. I deserve nothing. I deserve to let my mind rot in this godforsaken wasteland. Just be a stagnant soul like I was when I was alive. All my efforts in life, and look where they got me. My wife probably doesn't even care that I'm dead. Just a mild inconvenience for her.

Barry walks past me, his arm around the girl with baggy pants. He gives me a wink as they head to the backyard.

I walk outside to the front of the house. It's empty. Everyone on the property is either inside the house or in the backyard. Maybe they don't want to be seen by the other town folks. Hide their shame. Hide their pain. Hide the fact that they are here. Now that I notice, there are barely any windows in this house. The few that do exist are covered by a simple beige tarp.

The cacti are my only companions in the front yard. The only company I need in this place. Cacti are quite misunderstood. They're sharp, and they hurt, but they only use needles as a defense mechanism. You never hear of a cactus attacking someone in the same way you'd hear of a mountain lion or alligator attack. They have a sharp outside to protect their soft, fragile inside. They cannot talk, but they can listen. I don't have anything to say to them, though. The only audience I should have for my words is myself. I can't burden other people with my problems. They all have their own problems they have to deal with. It's nice to have the option though.

Who's taking care of these plants? On closer inspection, the cacti aren't doing so well. I'm pretty sure Andrew doesn't know that he even owns cacti.

I find an almost-full pail of water next to the wall and grab it. The handle breaks off as I lift it off the ground, and I trip when I try to grab the pail mid-air, falling forward and landing on my knees. Stagnant water splashes all over me and the ground. I look inside the pail and see that it is three-quarters empty now. Thankfully, no one saw that whole charade.

I get up and dust all the dirt off my pants. My pants are already ruined at this point, littered with holes here and stains there. I pick up the bucket by its sides and water the cacti in the front yard. Hopefully, it's enough until the next time someone waters them. Whenever that may be.

I'm going to take off from this place. Leave here without a trace. Say no goodbyes except to Barry. Maybe I can try to convince him to come with me. Help him escape from the fate that the house brings. Everyone else is too engulfed in sorrow to be convinced. They want to stay here. They're acclimated to it now. That's all they know. Don't know what else there is. The stories of their lives are just told as tall tales rather than past experiences. Telling their own stories as if they saw them on TV the night before – lives that they didn't experience but in fact only witnessed.

I re-enter the house, heading to the backyard to find Barry. As I pass through the front room, I notice that half of the people that had been in the house are missing, Andrew included. The rest are all kind of just standing or sitting there doing nothing except consuming their vices. I'm guessing they're the ones that have been here the longest. Their clothing is definitely the most dated. For them, the pleasure of this place is gone. They only stay because, at this point, it is all they know and they don't know how to change.

I look out the back door and find Barry laying on a chair with the girl from before on his lap, kissing him. I abruptly push open the back door, frightening both of them with the sudden sound. Barry almost throws the girl off of him with the sudden noise.

Barry looks agitated. "Jesus, man, you scared the hell out of me. What's up? What do you want?"

"Can I talk to you in private for a moment?" I ask.

"What? Chloe can't hear?"

"I prefer if it were just us two."

"Alright. You have horrible timing, though." Barry zips up his shorts. "Just glad you didn't come out here 30 seconds from now. Would've been a different scenario."

He grabs a cigarette from the girl, lights it, and walks over to me. "So, what's up? What's so important that it can't wait? Like Hank said, 'We got all the time in the world.'"

"I think I'm leaving this place. I think you should come."

Barry almost drops his cigarette from the news. "We just got here," he says as he readjusts his posture. "You mean, like this town or..." He motions around himself with his hands.

"I'm not sure, but I just want to get out of here. Specifically this house. This place isn't right for us. It's not really right for anyone. Except maybe Andrew. I mean, do you see some of the guests in this house?"

"Oh, I've definitely been looking at some guests here," Barry says, looking back at Chloe.

"Barry. I'm serious. Now's not the time to think with your pants. They're trapped in these vices. How truly miserable these people are underneath. It's fun and games for a little while, until it's not. I—"

"Look, man." Barry interjects. "I wasn't the most religious guy when I was alive. I've only been to church once, and that's only 'cause I was trying to get inside a church girl's pants. When I died, I thought there would be nothing. Just black, and that's it. Now look around at all this. This definitely wasn't what I was expecting. This all didn't come here by itself. It obviously came from some higher power. A higher power I didn't spend any time on Earth praying to or worshiping. What I heard about in church is that, when you die, you end up in Heaven if you were good or whatever. And let me tell you, despite all the alcohol here, I know this isn't Heaven. I'm blessed to be here, but I doubt there's anything better on the other side of my door for me. My cards are not in my favor to make that bet. My best bet is to just stay here."

"Life isn't just about being consumed by vices," I say to him. "Are you okay with just being stuck in this house?"

"This isn't life, though!" Barry yells. "We are not alive. So who cares? No one here cares, so why should you? What are you trying to fight, James? Seriously, what are you trying to accomplish?" Barry stands there for a second with a stern face, waiting for my response – a response which I didn't have.

His face and shoulders lower. "What do you want me to say? That I'm scared? That I don't want to know what's on the other side of that door? Those guys that are all part of this don't tell anyone here nothing and don't you think that's sketch?"

"Are you comfortable staying here for centuries and centuries? Do you want to be another Andrew Clark?" I ask.

"Yes, I am, and, yes, I do," Barry says confidently. "During the last few years of my life, my ambition was all about girls and partying, and what does this house bring me? Girls and partying. I had some troubles in my life, but, at the end of the day, I definitely tried to make the best of it. Now tell me this, James. Are you comfortable with yourself? Are you comfortable with anything?"

I am not comfortable with myself. At least I know that much.

I don't respond to his question, instead asking, "Wh-what about Mabel?"

"Yeah, what about her?" Barry's voice is dripping with attitude. "I'm dead, and she's alive. What's there to it? I'll see her in 60 years or so with her husband."

"I… I don't know," I say, defeated.

Barry takes a slow drag from his cigarette while staring at me. He exhales. "Goodbye, James. Was nice to meet you, and an interesting journey we had together. I hope you find the answers you're looking for."

I give him a faint "Goodbye." He turns and heads back to the girl on the chair. She joyfully waves goodbye to me. I give a half wave back.

This is the last time I will ever see Barry. I have no plans of coming back to this town, and he has no plans of leaving it. I haven't known him for long, but I know I won't ever forget the journey I had with him. No amount of alcohol can smear that memory away. I hope he could say the same. I wish him the best in this afterlife. I hope he truly enjoys it and isn't just masking away the pain like many here.

I open the back door and head through the living room. The same people that were there before are in the same spots doing the same activities. As I'm reaching for the front door, it swings open toward me. I jump back and Hank walks in. He is startled to find me standing right inside the door.

"Oh, sorry, James. Didn't mean to scare you. Just thought I'd come in for a bit and grab some beers and bum some stoges." Hank looks over my shoulder at the near-empty room. "But it looks like the party already moved to the back, which makes for an easy getaway. Say, do you want to crack a beer with me? Never fun drinking alone."

"Thanks, but I'm actually leaving."

"We can have some beers for the road. I don't like hanging out in this house much to be honest. Where are you headed? The Dive?"

"I'm not sure. I'm leaving this town and not coming back."

"Oh, you're *leaving* leaving," Hank says, surprised. "That was quick. Have any roadmaps for where you're headed?"

I think for a second. "Not sure. Got any suggestions?"

"Well, I'm pretty sure you don't want to go back through that sea to the south. So, tell you what friend, there's a station at the most northern point in town. That's actually how I came to this here town. The clerk there's name is Betty, and she owes me a favor. Tell her ol' Hank sent you, and she can get you on the train for free. I must warn, she's got a bit of a bite to her words."

"Thanks, Hank. I really appreciate it," I say.

"No problem. Since I'm getting you a free ticket outta town, I figure you could give me the rest of those tickets in your pocket. Not much use for them outside of here."

I hand him the rest of my drink tickets as he mouths the word "jackpot" to himself.

"Much obliged," he says, "If you're ever back in town, you know where to find me."

"Hey, could you do me a favor?" I ask him. "Could you keep an eye on Barry and make sure he's alright?"

"Sure can do. I'll make sure he don't get into too much trouble without me." Hank looks inside the kitchen. "If you'll excuse me, I see a cooler with my name on it."

He walks to the kitchen before stopping dead in his tracks and placing a finger in the air. "Oh. One more thing." He grabs one of the tickets and hands it to me. "Give that to Betty. She needs some sweetness in her life."

I grab the ticket and open the front door. I look back to see Hank opening up a cooler. "Goodbye, Hank," I say to him.

"Later, friend," he says, without deterring his attention from the cooler.

I step outside and slowly close the door behind me, hoping for a hand to stop it before it latches shut. Instead, the door creaks and whines until finally, it closes with a click. No hand meets the door. This is where my path splits away from everyone else's. I pass by the cacti garden and say goodbye to it. Though they don't respond back or show any expression, I can tell that they will miss me.

Chapter 9

I reach the northernmost point of town and find what I assume to be the train station. Everything is quiet and still, as if the entire place had been frozen in time. There's no interior; instead, the station consists of a single ticket booth on a platform with one track on each side of it. One track veers left into the horizon while the other veers off to the right. On one of the tracks, a train waits. I'm assuming this is the train I'll be leaving on. It's very old and rusted with writing on the side that is too faded to read. The only letters that aren't completely faded off are *A*, *T*, and *D*. I'd be surprised if this train could even operate.

I walk over to the lady in the booth. She is an older looking lady with gray hair that is frazzled like a bird's nest. She's wearing the exact same mid-gray nurse scrubs as Gary. She has a mole on her left cheek and a stare that could cut through glass.

I walk up to the window with her staring at every single movement I make.

"Hey the—"

"What do you want?" she barks in a low, raspy voice.

"Does your name happen to be Betty?"

She stares at me silently for a second, cold and expressionless. "Did Hank send you?" she finally asks.

"Yeah, how did you—"

"Here." She hands me a ticket through a slot in the glass.

"Thank you. Where does this ta—"

"Have a nice day."

I give her a nod to avoid being interrupted again. I slide the drink ticket through the glass slot. She grabs it swiftly and gives a sarcastic elongated "Thanks."

She stares at me as I walk past the booth, moving only her eyes and nothing else.

I look at the ticket. All it says is *Kroasic to Doyo Ruro*. I never knew the name of this town until now. No one had ever mentioned the name during my time here. No signs around the town. I guess I didn't really ask the name either. Now that I think of it, I didn't see any street signs either. How many people here actually know the name of this town? Does Andrew Clark even know? I guess it doesn't really matter, though. No one cares. Putting a name on something makes it all the more permanent to the mind.

I board the train and take a seat in the back. The train is completely silent. There's only about a half-dozen other people in the train car. Everyone is seated far apart from everyone else, quietly occupying themselves by sleeping or looking out the window. No one I recognize from the town.

The train blows its whistle, and the conductor comes onboard. He is a bulky white man with a thick beard. He looks over at me and gives me a smile and a tip of his hat. I return an awkward smile and wave my ticket in the air. He smirks and heads to the opposite side of the train, greeting the other passengers who are awake.

The brakes release and the wheels let out an unbearable shriek as the train starts to move. I cover my ears as it picks up speed. I look around and notice that no one else seems to mind the sound. As the train accelerates more and more, the screeching gradually fades. I look back and watch the town of Kroasic get smaller until it is just a minuscule speck in a desert plain. A speck that contains all the people I have met here. A haven in a barren desert. At least, that's what it looks like from afar.

Just like in the beginning of this journey, I am now alone. I'm sharing a train car with other people, but they might as well be miles away. Yet, at the same time, I'm not alone. My thoughts are constantly accompanied by me.

Hopefully, Doyo Ruro is a nice place. Maybe I won't feel the same way I felt back in the last town. Stuck in place. Stagnant. No feeling of moving forward. A melancholy tone to the place. No strive to make progress. What do I have to look forward to in my future if I always look into the past? I'm dead. What legacy do I leave? Losing my true love. Majoring in finance just to get a lowly job at a bank branch – a branch half a mile from the headquarters, where I *should* have been working. I shot for the stars and landed in the dumpster. My work has already forgotten about me. Only a minor inconvenience for them. Debra might have to work a few extra hours and through lunch for a week or two before they can find another expendable employee to take my place. What about my friends? What friends, though? I had considered them friends, but did they consider me the same? Why would anyone be friends with me? To them, I'm an acquaintance, if even that.

Maybe I'm so opposed to staying in the past because there has never been a time when I've been content in my past. No comfort. Except, of course, Jasmine. Jasmine, I hope you are well. I hope you found someone who didn't break your heart as I did. Someone who truly understands you. Hopefully, that person found your broken heart and glued it back together.

Our paths might cross again one day in this place. If so, I will say my apologies. I will tell you everything. The reason why. That's what you never received. An explanation. That's what you deserve. The only thing you expect from me. What you begged of me. Why I did it. That question probably kept soaring through your mind for years. Coming up with possible answers with no way to confirm them. Once all is said and done, I will say my goodbyes.

Are you here on this plain with me? I hope you are not. I hope you have many wonderful years ahead of you. I hope you don't end up here. Unfortunately, it seems everyone eventually ends up here. For a time, at least. In their own time.

I hear Hank's words: *Your door will find you.* How will it find me? When will it find me? Will it be months, years, centuries? How can they even track time here when it's permanently midday?

Why am I fighting this so hard? Why am I thinking like this? What really repelled me about that town? The stagnant nature of it, yes. But why? Why can't I be stagnant? Why can't I shut off this motor of progression? What progression, though? The progression I have is faux at best. A self-created hoax to calm my nerves. At least the people here seem to be real with themselves.

I could get a job. Seems there's jobs here for the people who want to work. I'm not sure if they have a stable currency system here, though. Seems to be more of a trading economy. At least in Kroasic.

Maybe I should head back to that little town in the desert. Maybe that was where my place was, and I didn't know. What if I don't have a place anywhere? Maybe I woke up just outside of that town for a reason. It's the place where those who don't belong go. I could hang out with Barry and Hank. Hang out in that house though? Barry will probably spend the majority of his time there. There or the bar. Maybe I could get adjusted to the house. At least I wouldn't be alone. Mentally maybe, but physically, I won't. Is it too late to—

"Ticket, please," a voice says to me.

I look up quickly to find the train conductor looming over me. In a friendly voice, he repeats, "Ticket, please." I hand him my ticket. He grabs it and puts on his glasses to read the small text.

"Ah, Doyo Ruro."

"Have you been?" I ask. "What's it like?"

"Oh, me? No, I haven't been there, but I know it will be just right for you."

"How so?"

He chuckles as he hands me back my ticket and turns away. "Oh, you'll see," he says. He passes by everyone else on the train without inspecting their tickets.

I wonder what he meant by that. Why does he assume this place will be just right for me? This guy might've been here a while. Knows how to read people and sees who comes from and leaves each town. Know who is where and how they are. So far, I haven't seen many roads or cars here. Trains must be the main form of transportation.

Then again, I was only in one small village. On one side of it is a hostile and barren desert, while, on the other side, there is a lone train station. That village is probably a dead end for a lot of people. Last stop of the line. A last resort. The Sea of Lost Souls, as Hank put it. The place where they go when they find nowhere else to be. Yet that is where I started. Am I heading somewhere or am I leaving somewhere?

Who am I to judge these people? Saying they are lost? I am the one who is lost. They actually seem rather content with where they are. I am not content no matter where I go. All my dreams could come true, and I would still not find happiness. What dreams does this place cause, though? Dreams that don't possess my head. Are there dreams that occupy my head? I haven't thought about them for a while. I just picture the dreams off in the corner, rusted and covered in dust. If I had any, they were probably only achievable when I was alive. Can't get a promotion here. Probably can't find Jasmine.

The only goal I could think of now is being content with myself. How is that possible? Where does it come from? Does it really come from oneself? Can no outside source manipulate your contentment if you locked it away in a windowless cell and threw away the key? No visitation allowed. Stuck in solitary confinement. No light. No sound. Just hope. Hope that someday, a light will come and take it away from this place. But deep down, it knows. It knows that light will not come. That its hope is pointless. Yet it still holds it. It still grasps onto hope no matter how hard you try to pull it away from it.

Do I have to take a side excursion to find inner peace first? What was a time when I was actually happy? With Jasmine, of course. But was I truly happy or are those false memories blurred by nostalgia and melancholy? No, those were good memories. I cannot corrupt them with my second-guessing thoughts. I remember the feeling when I was with her. How do I get those feelings back? Should I just forget about those memories? Should I just move on?

Yes, I should move on. But I can't forget those memories. Just loosen my grip on them. Rather than hold them tightly against my chest, I can place them on a bookshelf where I will come across them from time to time and appreciate them for what they are.

I need to close that chapter. Take it for what it is. Something I will no longer see, even if I yearn for it. Move on. Those words have never felt stronger than they do now. For once, I feel far away from my troubles. Even if it's for a second, I'm relieved.

The woman five rows in front of me is staring at chipped paint on her nails. Perhaps she's thinking about repainting them. Hiding the cracks from underneath. Possibly choosing a different color than before. Trying something different. Maybe something that'll get her out of her comfort zone. A bright neon color she's never considered.

There's a man on the other side of the car, who sits facing me with a briefcase on his lap. Perhaps he's looking to find someplace else to call home here, just like me. Can you call any part of this place home, though? Andrew Clark seems to be pretty acquainted with his house. His place even has a cacti garden.

I think it's just me. This place isn't terrible. It's just terrible for me. Or I'm just terrible. Maybe, on the other side of the door, there's no consciousness. Just the blackness that everyone fears. Or maybe people fear that their next stop is the bad place. What's the difference between here and Earth? Here, people can't die, because they already died. You can pursue what you were too scared to try on earth. Skydiving. Bungee jumping. Hang gliding. But I haven't seen any of that. Just overconsumption, vices, and people hanging around, waiting for nothing (which I assume a fair amount of them did when they were alive).

What about these people on the train? What are their plans? Are they traveling, finding a new place to take root? Possibly visiting loved ones from a different town? Setting out to pursue their ambitions? I haven't seen a map of the geological landscape of this area. How big is this mass of land we're on? Is it just a reconstruction of Earth or something completely different? I scan the inside of the car for a map of the rail system but find nothing. No ads or anything else. Only bare metal. It might've been on here at one point, only to be aged to dust by time. Even stagnant time ages you.

None of this matters. All this curious dialogue in my mind is just a distraction from the truth. Should I stay here in what they call the Sea of Lost Souls? Maybe I should—

All of a sudden, the train jerks back. The brakes wail once again, piercing through my eardrums and throwing me forward. Before we come to a complete stop, the train starts to accelerate again.

A barely intelligible, distorted voice starts speaking through the intercom overhead. A voice that only someone from New York would understand. "Sorry about that. Accidentally pressed the wrong lever."

An older woman on the other side of the train begins waving her frail, skinny arm in the air and yelling at the speaker above her. I see the train conductor leaving the driver's cart. As he passes through, he avoids the multiple sets of eyes that stare back at him with disdain.

Now the train is silent again besides the wheels moving below me. The people who were disrupted and annoyed moments ago have gone back to the activities that had previously occupied them. Sleeping. Staring. I believe one person is crocheting now.

I wonder what my wife is doing right now on Earth. I can't even call her my wife anymore. She's my widow. 'Til death do us part,' like that woman said. She's probably living life as we speak. Probably put on a grand spectacle at my funeral. Crying, yelling, throwing herself on top of my casket. She always loves being the center of attention, even at the most inappropriate of times. She could've been a good actor if she had decided to go that route. Maybe she'll give it a try now. No anchor holding her back in New York anymore.

I honestly couldn't care less though. She didn't care about me, and, as a result, I showed her no emotions in return. It was a loveless marriage. Loveless from the beginning. Both of us pressured to marry the other by our parents. I shouldn't hate her. She was put into the same situation I was. She's the only one that truly understands me, and now, no one truly understands her. I hope she's still on Earth, and, when she comes here, she doesn't end up lost like me.

People don't find themselves in a place. They find themselves inside themselves. They just have to look past the skin and bone and into the soul.

I should probably rest. I haven't rested much since I got here. I'm quite exhausted but not as exhausted as I'd expect after being up for what I assume to be days. I close my eyes and quickly drift off.

Chapter 10

I wake up to the sound of the horrible screeching once again. I press on my ears and sit up, suddenly noticing that the train car is completely empty. Everyone had been here before I fell asleep. Where did they go? The old woman scolding at the intercom, gone. The man who had been motionless since I boarded the train, gone. Maybe they jumped off when I wasn't looking. Got off at a stop while I was taking my nap. Hard to sleep through those brakes, though. Maybe they switched cars. Had issues with being in this one.

I look out the window. All I see is complete nothingness. Just an empty plain on either side of the train as it slows down. No evidence of human influence for miles besides the tracks underneath me. Why are we stopping here? It doesn't look like there's anything that resembles any sort of town. Maybe some unlucky individual ended up arriving here and the train is picking them up to give them a lift into town. But where are the other passengers?

The train finally comes to a complete stop. I sit there in silence for a few minutes. The quiet swish of my pants rubbing against the seat fabric is the only noise throughout the entire car. Maybe something is blocking the rails. Or maybe the rails are broken up ahead so we're stuck until a repair crew can come out.

The door swings open behind me. I snap my head back so fast that I almost get whiplash. Looking down at me is the train conductor with the thick beard. A faint smile flashes across his otherwise expressionless face.

"Well, I believe this is your stop," he says to me.

I look at him, confused. "Where are we?" I ask as I rub my neck.

"Your stop, like I just said."

"But I thought I was headed to a town. To Doyo Roro, like it says on my ticket."

He chuckles and puts his hand on my shoulder. "This is Doyo Roro. We overshot our stop, and it's a few cars back." He takes his arm off my shoulder and extends it to me. "Come. Walk with me. It'll all make sense momentarily."

"What do you mean? What is Doyo Roro?"

He raises his flat palm out toward me. "Can't disclose that."

I get up and follow him through multiple train cars. I look through the windows of the rundown train and see nothing but empty plains on either side. Each train car we pass through is completely empty.

"Where are all the other passengers?" I ask, confused.

Without turning back, he says, "This isn't their stop."

The conductor opens the door to the next car. "Ahh, here is the right car."

I hesitate, watching to see what he does. He walks to the middle of the car, stopping next to the exit doors. He fumbles with his keys until he finds the right one. "Aha!" He unlocks the door and swings it open with great force. He looks back surprised to see that I'm still at the end of the car. He waves me over. "Well, come on, it's not gonna hurt you."

"*It?*" I ask as I walk over to the conductor.

"Well, I wish you luck," he says with a tip of his hat.

"Thanks?" I say. "Say, I never got your name."

"They call me Tom for some reason," he says, gesturing toward the door.

I exit and walk down the steps, pausing on the last one. Below me, I see dry, cracked dirt. I lower both my feet onto the waterless soil. The door behind me slams shut. I look back to see Tom waving goodbye with a friendly smile and another tip of his hat. I turn around and look up to see what faces me – what Doyo Roro truly is. Standing there, ten feet in front of me, was a mid gray door with the initials of *J.D. above* it.

Thank you for finishing my book. I really appreciate it and am thankful you took time out of your day to read it. If you feel you wish to leave a review, whether good or bad, it would mean a lot to me.

Brett Nolan is an author based out of San Jose, CA. When he isn't writing stories, he is making music for the music groups AnotherMay, Motels At Midnight, and Designation.

If you want to hear more about Brett Nolan, please visit BrettaNolan.com